Unwanted Guest

Gary McPherson

Charlotte, North Carolina

This novel is a work of fiction. Names, characters, places, and incidents are either products of the author's imagination or used fictitiously. All characters are fictional, and any similarity to people living or dead is purely coincidental.

Chapter One

O liver smacked the bottom of his tact light with his palm. The bulb flickered in the void. He smacked it again, and a beam brightened the basement. Graffiti and an upside-down pentagram were spray painted on the moldy white wall. The poorly painted symbols only looked a couple of days old. Oliver cocked his head and listened. His heartbeat and shallow breaths were all he heard.

A faint scratching sound caught his attention. Oliver aimed his light in that direction. A mouse busily chewed on something between its claws. Oliver's eyes widened, and he took several steps back until he stood in a doorway. A cold breeze passed through his body, and he shivered. Anxious to get away from the mouse and the draft, he entered the room.

More moldy white walls surrounded him. Rotted carpet covered the concrete floor. A cracked window atop the wall allowed the shadows outside to dance about Oliver. One shadow appeared to move in the opposite direction and into the closet.

He blinked and mumbled, "Get a hold of yourself. This isn't your first investigation."

Oliver walked to the center of the room. He placed his EMF meter on the floor and walked to the far wall from the doorway.

Oliver spoke forcefully, "If there is anyone here with me, make your presence known. Walk over to that green light. When you do, other lights will turn on."

He cut off his flashlight. A green light flickered, and an intermittent buzz faded in and out.

"Just move closer."

The buzzer increased to a high pitch. It sporadically cut on and off, like a scream. All the lights remained off except for the yellow one in the center.

Oliver hollered, "Please back up."

The lights danced, first left to right and then right to left. The speaker buzzed like an angry bee. Oliver could feel his hair standing on end.

"I said back up!"

The room became still.

"Can you make a noise?"

Oliver rhythmically knocked against the wall, "Shave and a Haircut."

Nothing happened.

Frustrated, he blurted out, "You can mess with my equipment but not knock on the wall?"

Oliver's mouth curved down, "It must have been a malfunction." He turned on his flashlight and started towards the EMF meter. The lights jumped to red. Startled, Oliver took a step back, and the lights turned off. He took a step forward, and the meter lit up and remained on. He took two steps back, and the meter returned to a single green light.

Oliver sighed, "Great, another thing I have to fix."

He walked over, and the meter remained nominal. He picked it up, turned it off, and slid it into his pant's pocket. He reached into his coat pocket and pulled out a wrinkled piece of paper.

Oliver mumbled, "Let's see, the basement bedroom is a bust. The playroom had a scary rodent. Somebody said they found a pile of dirt behind a storage door they thought might be a grave. There's always a pile of dirt behind a finished basement with a grave, so I think I'm done down here."

Putting away his notes, Oliver prepared to move to the main floor. He reached the bottom of the steps when he heard the house's front door open. He could hear several footsteps scampering on the floor above him and then up the stairs. He knew the dilapidated steps were hazardous to climb, much less sprint. He scribbled on his paper, "Echo upstairs?" He slipped away from the basement steps and returned to the empty room.

Oliver whispered to himself, "Maybe it's an echo. Just a sound from the past. That's all. But what if it's squatters?"

He paced in a tight circle around the room. Finally, Oliver pulled out his phone and dialed the one person he knew he could count on.

A familiar voice answered, "Hello?"

Oliver whispered, "Jimmy, it's Ollie. I'm at the old Hollister house."

"What?" yelled Jimmy. "Are you nuts? You should never investigate that place alone."

Oliver walked to the far corner and whispered, "I know. Look, man, I think someone is in the house with me. Could be squatters."

Jimmy's voice trembled slightly. "Is it somebody or something?"

Oliver took a long slow breath, "Jimmy, don't talk like that. I heard the front door open and a lot of footsteps. I can't call the cops; I'm trespassing. Can you just come over? I'm in the bedroom in the basement. You know, the place you told me about."

"Wait, what if people are on the first floor and hear me come in?"

Oliver forgot about the mouse in the other room and slid his back down the wall. "Man, I'm an idiot. The basement door is unlocked. That's how I got into this place. I can slip out the same way. Hang on a minute."

Getting to his feet, he quickly rushed towards the darkness and the unlocked door. The dusty, painted door was closed just as he left it.

He put the phone to his ear, "Jimmy, I should be fine."

There was no answer.

"Jimmy? You there?"

Oliver shrugged and dropped the phone into his pants pocket. The flashlight started to flicker, and he slapped it.

"Come on, man, not you again."

The light began to fade, and the door disappeared in the dying light. Oliver yanked the door, but it would not move. He put his foot against the wall and tried again.

Thunk. Oliver rubbed his shoulder and hoped the door had loosened from the painful impact. Once more, it failed to open. He was about to break the glass with his flashlight but was worried about the noise and stopped.

Oliver heard the basement door creak open. Footsteps descended the staircase. Oliver held his breath and prayed silently that he would avoid discovery. Darkness overtook the gray shadows in the empty room on the far side of the basement. Oliver squinted, and a carbon-colored mist darkened the shadowed room.

Beads of sweat trickled down his forehead. Oliver tried not to breathe. Carefully, his hand gripped the door handle. Deliberately, Oliver turned the knob for all he was worth. He prayed silently and gave a slow tug. Nothing happened.

He attempted to release the door, but his sweaty palms stuck to the old brass knob. It gave a quiet rattle as Oliver removed his hand. A pair of glowing white eyes across the basement appeared, staring directly at Oliver.

Chapter Two

J im hollered, "Ollie, are you there? Say something."

He desperately text, "RU OK?"

After several seconds the phone returned an error, and the message remained unsent. Jim bolted for his coffee table and grabbed his jacket and truck keys. Fighting to put his jacket on, he rushed down the hall, bounced off a wall, and into his bedroom.

Digging around his nightstand, he found a container of holy water and his wallet. He hurried out of his apartment, winced, and stopped to rub his leg after locking the door. His eyes widened, and he sighed. Looking longingly at the elevator, he turned towards the stairs and ran down the three flights. He quickly hobbled to his truck, leaned against it, and forced himself to the door.

The old F150's door screeched in protest as he flung it open. The dome light behind the bench seat cast a drab illumination for Jim to organize himself.

He held up his phone, "Call David."

"Calling David."

Jim grunted and pushed himself into the driver's seat with one leg. He closed the door, and the engine roared to life before the phone could be heard ringing through the speaker. When David answered, Jim was pulling out of his apartment's parking lot.

"Dave, it's Jim."

David sounded annoyed, "Hey man, I told you before I can hardly hear you when you call from your truck."

Jim squealed the tires as he turned onto First Street, heading for the highway. His voice pitched upward, "Look, I don't have time to explain. Oliver is at the old house alone, and I think he's in trouble."

"What old house? Jim, talking high and faster isn't helping me out. Slow down. What old house?"

Jim took a long slow breath and eased off the accelerator, "Okay. Oliver told me he was trying to get out of the Hollister House. Something about hearing somebody upstairs. The basement door was jammed, and then his phone went dead."

There was silence for a few seconds, and Jim thought maybe he had lost signal. Then David's calm voice came over the speaker, "Okay. This could be bad. Look, I'm out of town on business. I won't be back until late tomorrow night. I'm afraid the only thing I can do is pray. Do you have any holy water?"

Jim nodded to himself, "Yea. In my jacket. What if it's a person, though? I hate to call the cops. I mean, it isn't like it's legal to be inside there, even if it is abandoned."

David responded in a firm voice, "If you get there and see anyone, and I mean anyone near the house, you call the cops. A trespassing warning is nothing if Oliver is in trouble. You can't take on some methhead on your own."

Jim frowned, "Okay. I'm almost at the exit. I need to get focused. Pray hard for us. I have no idea what I'm walking into."

David answered, "God, watch over my brothers. Give us wisdom concerning Oliver, amen."

Jim began to press the red button on his screen, "See ya."

He hit the button and tossed the phone on the seat. Jim guided the truck onto the offramp and then headed left. The homes in the neighborhood were large. It was hard to imagine why the old home's owner did not tear down the decrepit mansion. It could easily be replaced with a shiny new McMansion or two.

Rumors claimed the land was cursed, and the owner could not find a buyer. Others had said the owner was an old widow who could not let go of the estate even though she no longer lived there.

Whatever the reason was, the house had a reputation among neighbors and curious trespassers alike. The large gray mansion was to be avoided at all costs. Although transients occasionally tried their luck, they always ran away before sunrise. Jim guessed it was the reason the neighbors never complained to the city. Vagrancy was a short-termed problem, if it was a problem at all regarding the property.

Suddenly the truck jolted, sputtered, and jerked. Jim threw it in neutral and coasted to the curb. The engine knocked horribly when he cut it off. A frown passed over his face as he reached under the seat for his flashlight.

He unlatched the hood, turned on his flashlight, and exited the truck. In the distance, under the streetlights, he could see the black entrance to his destination. He started to walk towards it but then turned and opened the hood. At first glance, everything seemed in order.

A smile crossed Jim's face when he spied a wire hanging from the distributor cap. He slid it back into place, closed the hood, and returned to the truck.

The old pickup roared back to life. He took in all of the dark houses on the block. People were sound asleep, unaware of what might be happening just a few yards from their bedrooms.

Small segments of the old house were barely visible from the street as Jim pulled in. It did not sit too far from the road. Jim eased his way through the inky air with only his parking lights on in case someone else was in the old dwelling.

Oliver's Ford Ranger was parked next to the house, near the backyard. It was more or less out of sight from anyone not looking for a vehicle in the driveway. Jim turned off the truck, grabbed his flashlight, leaned over to the glove box, and opened it.

A handgun and EMF reader sat inside the bare steel space. He reached for both but only grabbed the pistol and closed the glovebox. He expertly slid the pistol into its waist holster.

"Get ahold of yourself. You're just here to grab Ollie and get out."

Jim silently opened the truck door, slid out, and gently closed it back. His eyes adjusted to the darkness around him. The old tree limbs hung like phantoms inside shadows. Jim moved slowly, easing his foot down onto the leaf litter with each step.

He headed towards the side of the house near the truck. When he got to a set of steps, he stopped and listened. Everything was dead quiet. Jim turned on his flashlight and could see where someone had cleared off the steps leading to the basement earlier. He hoped that it was Oliver. He eased down the stairs and tried the door, but it was locked. Shining his light through the window, Oliver was nowhere to be seen. Jim started to holler his name and knock on the door but then thought better of it.

Turning off his flashlight, he quietly made his way to the front of the house. Faded police tape that once covered the front door had been torn away, and the plywood that covered the doorway had been removed. The dry rotted front door hung open. Jim took a step inside and listened but heard nothing.

He slowly backed out of the doorway, down the steps, and back to his truck. Jim knelt down and dialed 911.

"911, what's your emergency?"

"This is James Monroe. I am at 1300 Maple Dr. in Hopewell. I think someone has broken into the abandoned house. My friend's truck is here, and he's missing. Can I get an officer?"

"Oh, it's you, Jim. This is Bernice. Robert is patrolling over there tonight. I've already sent him on a couple of domestics. I'll have him drive by in a little bit."

Jim's voice whispered urgently, "Please, sooner than that. It's Oliver. He was over here by himself. Someone busted through the plywood in the front, but Oliver couldn't escape through the basement door. I tried getting in that way, but it's locked. I'm not sure Oliver is alone."

"I understand. I'll get Robert over there ASAP."

Jim gave a sigh of relief, "Thank you."

Chapter Three

Jim hunkered down behind his truck and mumbled, "You can't just hide here like a coward. What if Oliver's hurt? Suppose someone attacked him, or worse?"

He eased his way back inside the cab and grabbed a small ammo box from under the seat. He slipped it silently into his pocket. After ensuring the gun was well hidden in the waist holster under his shirt, Jim walked confidently back to the front door. He stepped inside. Decrepit stairs rose to his left, and paint and wallpaper hung in pieces.

Jim put his hand behind his back and hollered, "Ollie, you in here?"

A scratching sound from the parlor caused Jim to turn on his flashlight. A mouse scurried from view.

Jim tried again, "Ollie, you need to holler or something. Tell me where you are."

The sound of a single footstep from the back of the entryway caught Jim's attention. Two glowing white eyes appeared, and Jim angled his flashlight in their direction. A stocky man with gray eyes stared back at him before shielding himself from the flashlight's beam.

"Do you mind? Who are you? Why are you here?"

Jim lowered the light away from his eyes and scanned the stranger's body. A tight, dirty t-shirt barely hid the man's small gut. An old, faded pair of blue jeans hung loosely, and a couple of crusty work boots finished the man's ensemble. Jim noticed a gun in his other hand and immediately drew his weapon from its holster.

Jim blinded the stranger once more. "Put down your weapon. I'm armed and have mine aimed at your chest."

At the sound of a thud, Jim lowered his beam to see the gun on the floor.

"Kick it to me."

"You some sort of cop?" asked the stranger.

The man kicked the gun in Jim's direction, and Jim holstered his pistol.

He ignored the man's question and asked his own. "What's your name?"

"Call me John. You know, John Smith."

A smile appeared on John's face, putting a shiver down Jim's spine.

"Okay, John. There was a man in here tonight. His name is Oliver."

John queried, "What's his last name?"

"Not your problem. I know he's still here because his truck is in the driveway."

John nodded, "Yea, well, he's my problem. Your friend is snooping around where he doesn't belong."

Jim could feel beads of sweat forming on his forehead. "I can say the same for you. This isn't your place."

John cocked his head, "Is it yours?"

Jim slowly shook his head.

"Then I call squatters rights."

Jim raised his right hand and rested it outside his rear pocket. "I'm not here to play games. I want my friend, and we'll be on our way."

John reached into his pocket and pulled something out. The sliding blade made a distinct noise as it locked into place. He started cleaning his fingernails. "That's not what your friend told me. He won't say a word. I'm not sure he's blinked. I found him in the basement, all wild-eyed. I thought maybe he took some bad drugs."

"He doesn't do drugs."

John put the knife away, "Well, he needs help. I don't know what his problem is, but I don't want the attention. Just do me a favor. You never saw me, and he's all yours."

Jim didn't respond, and John went back into the darkness, where Jim knew the kitchen was located. He heard John groan, and, in a minute, he came out holding Oliver up.

Jim took a step and then stopped himself. "Ollie, can you walk?"

At the sound of Jim's voice, Oliver blinked and pushed himself off John.

"Who are you?" asked Oliver.

"Nobody, go to your friend."

Oliver quickly walked over to Jim and hugged him. Jim held Oliver only for a second before pushing him away. A noise on the second-floor walkway made all three men look up. Jim pointed his flashlight and saw a gaunt, pale woman with hollow eyes looking down.

She spoke with a raspy voice, "Johnny, I thought you said I was done for the night. I can't take two men at once. I need my sleep. Send them away."

Jim replied, "We were just going."

The woman walked away, and John started in Jim and Oliver's direction.

Jim pulled his pistol once more, "Don't move."

John stopped.

Jim continued, "You can have your gun after we leave, but if you so much as peek your head out that front door before we've left, I'll blow it off."

John appeared to grind his teeth. He finally said, "Remember, you saw nothing. You know what snitches get."

Jim nodded and backed Oliver and himself out of the house and down the stairs. Jim held his gun as he and Oliver ran to the truck.

From behind, John yelled, "Hey, a little something to keep you honest."

Oliver dove to the ground, and Jim spun around, got down on his knee, winced, and leveled his pistol. Blue and red lights pulsed in the darkness behind Jim. A muzzle flash appeared in the dark doorway in front of him, and Jim heard a bullet whistle by his head and struck his truck. Car tires slid to a stop.

Over an intercom came a voice, "This is the police. Put down your weapons."

Both men tossed their guns and got on the ground without being asked. The sound of the policeman's footsteps grew closer.

Jim whispered, "Robert, It's me, Jim. I got Ollie. He was being held against his will."

Robert replied, "Just stay there, don't move."

The policeman passed both men and headed straight to John. After putting him in handcuffs, he hollered, "Okay, he's in custody."

Jim and Oliver stood up and brushed themselves off. John glared at Jim.

John's voice was almost a growl, "What did I tell you about snitching?"

Robert interrupted, "You have the right to remain silent. I suggest you use it. Oliver, why did this guy kidnap you?"

Oliver shrugged, "I can't remember much of anything after I called Jimmy."

John jerked his arm from Robert and spoke up, "Wait a minute. I'm no kidnapper. I found this guy hiding in the basement, looking all freaked out. I thought he had a bad trip and brought him upstairs into the kitchen. He wouldn't take any water or anything. Just sat there."

Robert looked at Oliver, "Is that true?"

"I don't know. Could be. I don't remember anything. I was doing my investigation in the basement. I heard footsteps upstairs and tried to escape through the basement door because I thought someone was in the house. I don't remember anything after that."

Robert sat John on the porch and then examined Oliver's head. "Huh, no bumps or bruises. Do you have any pain?"

"No."

Robert stepped back, "Alright, well, I know how to get hold of both of you. You're free to go, but I will need statements later."

John tapped his right foot, "So, you guys work for the cops?"

Robert answered, "In a manner of speaking. They investigate ghosts, demons, and paranormal stuff. You'd be surprised what we hear about on the job."

John looked down at the porch, "Great, Scooby and the gang are looking into the one empty house I picked."

Jim and Oliver started toward their cars. Behind them, Robert said, "So, why don't you tell me why you shot my friend's truck?"

Jim reached for Oliver as he started for his truck. "Hey, you okay to drive?"

Oliver responded in a quiet voice, "Sure. I'll come over tomorrow and tell you what happened."

Jim whispered back, "I thought you didn't remember anything."

Oliver answered, "Tomorrow."

Jim backed out and followed Oliver down the street. Two more police cruisers with their emergency lights on passed by them and headed for the empty house.

Chapter Four

Oliver clutched the left side of his head and held his phone to his right ear. Half a cup of lukewarm coffee sat next to his laptop on the kitchen table. He squeezed his eyes shut and waited for Jim to answer.

"Jim."

Oliver croaked, "Hey man, it's Oliver."

"Ollie, what's going on? You sound pretty rough."

Oliver cleared the phlegm from his throat, "Yea, I feel like I partied hard last night."

"Did you?"

"You know me better than that." He bent down slightly and turned his head.

Jim asked, "Look, after what you went through, I would have downed a few beers. Are you up to coming over today?"

Oliver whispered, "Yea. Let me take a Tylenol or something, and give me a couple of hours."

"I have a better idea. I'll just come by your place later."

Oliver mumbled, "Okay."

He hung up the phone, dropped it on the table, and downed the last of his coffee. Oliver stood, swayed, and then stumbled to the bathroom. After finding some pain medicine, he walked into his apartment's living room and collapsed on the couch.

The sound of his doorbell roused him out of a dead sleep. His headache was duller.

Oliver mumbled, "Hang on."

He stood and stumbled a few steps before rubbing the sleepiness away from his eyes and answering the door. Jim stood there with a grin on his face and a greasy sack of burgers from Oliver's favorite burger joint.

Jim said, "I know it isn't a hangover, but it might help anyway."

"Can't hurt."

Jim stepped inside and headed for the kitchen table, "Are you feeling any better?"

"Yea, compared to this morning, I'm fine."

"Good."

Jim tore into the bag and pulled out their burgers and fries. Oliver grabbed a couple of colas from his refrigerator. For the next fifteen minutes, neither man said a word as they devoured their food.

Oliver pushed his chair back, "Man, I was hungrier than I thought."

"Me too."

After several seconds Oliver finally spoke, "I guess we should talk about last night."

Jim held up his hand, "Before we do, I need to understand something. Why did you go alone? The first rule of investigating is to have a buddy with you. Last night proves why that's so important."

Oliver played with his dirty paper napkin, "I know. It's just, well, ever since Tracy died, I have questions."

"About what? God? Your Faith? Ghosts?"

Oliver leaned towards Jim, "All of it. Let's be real. Nobody in our church or most churches understands this stuff. They either say to have faith, which is their way of saying don't bother looking for answers, or they claim everything we see on earth is demonic. Heck, half the elders claim what we do is evil."

Jim looked up at the ceiling as he spoke, "Yea, I know. They seem to forget all the verses about Jesus taking on demons or the disciples thinking he was a ghost, especially after the resurrection. I get your frustration but look, Tracy was a Christian. Wherever he is, we'll all be together in heaven one day. I assume you still believe that much."

Oliver shrugged, "Maybe. I mean, he was our age and a righteous dude. He was better than the two of us put together. Every other word was Jesus with him. The guy deserved to be in the movies if he was acting."

"That's a fact."

"Then why did God kill him?"

Jim looked Oliver in the eye, "There it is—the death card. Maybe God doesn't consider dying in this world as death. Remember the whole second death Jesus mentions?"

Oliver sat back, "I know all that. Still, what about the things we've seen? The spirits we run into when we investigate. Are the elders right? Is everything a demon?"

Jim's brow wrinkled, "You know it isn't."

"Right. So, what is it? Let's say it's people's ghosts. Are the people going to heaven and waiting, or are the people going to hell? Is it what Roman Catholics considered purgatory? Why would God allow people who suffered in an asylum to remain there after they died?"

Jim's brow creased, "I really don't know. We've always focused on what sort of paranormal activity a location has and removing any demons if the owners ask us. We've never considered the real reason why the spirits are there."

Oliver rolled up his napkin and threw it into the trashcan at the edge of the kitchen. "Two points." He looked back to Jim, "Exactly. I want to know. That old house is one of the most haunted locations we've ever been inside."

Jim interrupted, "And we know there's a demon there."

Oliver waved him off, "We think there is. We never took the time to test the spirits in the house. I thought maybe I could ask who they were and why they were there. You know, find out some answers."

Jim reached over and grabbed Oliver's wrist, "Do not consult with the dead. You know that. You know how dangerous that can be. If it is a demon disguised as a spirit, they could attach themselves to you. Promise me you won't do that."

Oliver pulled away from Jim's grip. "Yea, I mean, I know. After last night I won't take it that far."

"What happened last night that you couldn't tell me with Robert there?"

"Remember that dude, John? Let's just say I might want to consider acting."

Jim asked, "You weren't frozen in fear?"

Oliver chuckled for a moment, "Oh, I was scared out of my mind, but I didn't freak out. I just acted freaked out. Let me tell you what happened.

"My phone lost signal and then went dead. I tried to loosen the door, but it didn't work. I sat there without making a sound. I saw a black shadow pass along the wall and into the bedroom. Then it turned around, and I saw these glowing white eyes. It was super weird. Anyway, he saw me and came in my direction.

"As the thing glided towards me, it appeared to start walking, and my flashlight came on. I pointed it at the figure; lo and behold, it was John. I saw his gun and decided that acting like a frightened idiot was the best option. He got me to the kitchen, and I was there maybe two minutes before you two interacted."

Jim rubbed his chin and tapped his fingers on the table. He finally looked up, "So, are you saying we let a demon loose in Robert's jail?"

Oliver shrugged, "Beats me. It was like he was possessed, but I can't tell you where John ended, and the demon began."

"And you let Robert take him into custody and left him there. No warning?"

Oliver grimaced, "No. That isn't how I saw it. It's obvious the demon doesn't want to be seen. I think it let me live because he assumed I was too freaked out to say anything. Besides, he doesn't know I saw him in the basement. Think about what happened when you two interacted. John was in charge when he shot your truck. A demon would have killed both of us. By the way, sorry about the truck. I guess John thought we needed some convincing to stay quiet."

"Not your fault. Fortunately, John only hit the bed. I touched up the paint around the hole. I kind of like it. A souvenir of our adventures together."

Oliver said, "Okay. We need to talk to Robert and find out what happened to John. We also need to try to keep the girls away from him."

Jim clenched his fist, "You mean his sex slaves. I hate human trafficking. I can't believe they'd let the girls return to that monster."

"Just the same, let's find out. If John goes back to the house, and I think he will, we can't do anything if he has anyone else there. That's like a hostage situation, and that's way outside our expertise."

Jim agreed, "Yea, I'll set up a meeting with Robert, and we can get the info."

Oliver stood up, "I'll call Dave. We're going to need a demonologist."

Jim stood with him and headed towards the door. "Well, he's out of town until tonight. I'll call him when I get the meeting time, and we can all get together at once."

Jim was about to walk out of the door but stopped and turned to Oliver, "Quick question, why do you think John will return to the house?"

Oliver answered, "I don't know. I mean, we both think there was a demon at the house. If there was, it possessed John for a reason. It would have already left if it was trying to hitch a ride in John's body."

Jim leaned against the doorjamb, "We need to get this figured out."

Oliver nodded as Jim let himself out of the door.

Chapter Five

Oliver sat quietly in Jim's pickup with his arms crossed and hands clinched. He stared down at the dusty, cracked dashboard and took long, slow breaths. Jim had his favorite nineteen-eighties country music mix playing on the radio via Bluetooth from his phone. Oliver's shoulder bounced off the passenger window with each bump in the road.

"Why so uptight?"

Oliver glanced at Jim and back at the dash, "I know I screwed up, and now I have to confess it to the team."

Oliver felt Jim's hand grip his shoulder, "Cheer up. This isn't an inquisition. I've briefed Jaimie and David. David will probably give you a hard time, but you know how he is. Mr. Serious, even at a party. If it helps, I told him to back off giving you a lecture because you'd learned your lesson."

Oliver let his hands relax, "Thanks, man. I feel like an idiot. I should have come to you first. It's just, well, you know, we were the three musketeers all through school. Now there's a void that can't be filled."

Jim nodded and wiped a tear from his cheek.

Oliver continued, "After Tracy died, I was almost afraid to get together. It felt like I might lose you too."

"Thanks, that explains the cold shoulder. Ollie, we aren't going anywhere until God says it's our time. So, let's make the most of what we've been given. Besides, who knows? In ten years, we could be in different jobs on the other side of the country from each other."

Oliver looked out at the passing forest, "You're right."

The sign for the park entrance came into view. Jim turned off the road and headed for the covered picnic areas. Oliver pointed at David's black Tahoe, already parked near a picnic table where he sat.

Oliver muttered, "The beast waits for his prey."

Jim chuckled.

As soon as the truck stopped, Oliver got out of the cab. He walked ahead at a steady pace. As soon as he reached the picnic table, the two shook hands. "Dave, good to see you."

David's other hand came up without a word and began throwing water at Oliver. It only made the humid summer day wetter. Then a streak of water hit his right eye. Oliver jerked his head back and turned away from David.

David asked, "Does it burn?"

Oliver's voice was gruff, "No, duh, you hit me right in the eye with that stuff. You know it's salt water."

David answered, "Quit crying. It's less than you get in the ocean."

"You hit me in the eye."

David responded, "That was the idea. Maybe now you'll think twice. What if you had an attachment? You have no idea how you would respond to the holy water."

Jim interrupted, "Dave, I asked you to take it easy."

"I did."

Oliver blinked a few more times and then sat down, "And that's why I won't go into demonology. You guys are way too intense."

"The devil's intense."

Oliver and Jim answered in unison, "We know."

David reached for a paper towel from his back pocket and handed it to Oliver. Looking around, Oliver noticed the park was empty. A heat index of ninety was a little too toasty for the folks in this Carolina Mountain community.

Jim asked, "Has anybody heard from Jaimie?"

David shook his head.

"Well, I'll give her a couple more minutes. Robert is going to join us before too long."

David cocked his head, "So, law enforcement is finally joining us?"

Jim answered, "This time. Robert's a friend of ours. You've met him."

David nodded, "Oh, yeah, nice guy."

The sound of tires turning into the park caught the group's attention. Oliver smiled at Jaimie's bright pink Jeep Wrangler that came skidding to a stop next to the other vehicles. She hopped out of her car. Oliver dared not blink as he stared at her red mid-drift, white running shorts, and ponytail. All the men stood, and Jaimie waived and jogged her way to the group.

Before anyone could say a word, she dove into Oliver. Instinctively he nuzzled into her neck. She smelled like fresh wildflowers. Jaimie gave him such a hard squeeze he could hardly breathe. They released, and Oliver giggled before he could stop himself.

Jaimie asked, "Are you okay?"

"Yea. I just sort of lost who I was for a couple of days. Nothing bad happened to me."

David spoke up, "Nothing bad? A sex slaver kidnaps you, and nothing bad happened?"

Oliver shrugged as he looked into Jamie's dark eyes, "It was nothing. Jim came and saved me. We musketeers never let each other down."

Jamie walked over and gave Jim a kiss on his cheek, "Thank you."

Jim blushed and gave Jaimie a nod.

David shook his head and sat down, "Empaths."

Jaimie sat down next to Oliver across from David and asked, "What's wrong with us?"

David rolled his eyes, "Oh, nothing, I suppose. Don't get me wrong; you're super valuable when an investigation is happening, but a huge liability when we come across a dark spirit."

"Why is that?"

David answered, "Um, how do I put this? People are naturally attracted to empaths because they are compassionate."

Oliver interjected, "What's wrong with that?"

David looked at Oliver, "There's nothing wrong with it, but they also attract spirits. Sometimes the spirits are dark. If they aren't careful, they can end up with an attachment, or worse, if they don't know Jesus."

Jaimie leaned forward and looked David straight in the eyes, "But I do."

David leaned back, "I know. Look, let Oliver tell us what happened. I'm concerned for the whole team. Spirits and gangsters are not a good mix."

Jaimie leaned on her elbow and looked into Oliver's eyes. His head felt light.

"Well," said Jamie. "I'm waiting."

Oliver cleared his throat, and Jim interrupted, "Wait, Robert is pulling in."

The team saw the police cruiser pull into a parking space. Officer Roberts was dressed for work and looked all business except for the Subway bag in his hand. He approached the team, shook hands with everyone, and sat down at the table. Robert immediately opened his bag and unwrapped his sandwich.

Jamie asked, "Did you bring enough for everyone?"

Robert looked around red faced with a piece of stringed lettuce hanging out of his mouth. He worked to poke it in and mumbled, "Sorry."

David spoke up, "Nobody said anything about food."

Robert took a hard swallow, "Sorry, it's my dinner break. If I don't eat now, I have another six hours before my shift ends."

Jim jumped in, "Oliver, go ahead and tell everyone what you saw."

Oliver cleared his throat again, "Well, I'm not sure what I'd call it. It had to be a demon, and I'm sure it possessed this John fellow who held me at gunpoint. I was down in the basement, trying not to be seen. I heard footsteps heading into the basement, and my instincts told me it was a person because they sounded so heavy, and the boards creaked under their weight.

"At first, I saw an enormous black shadow at least seven feet tall. It passed into the bedroom and then turned in my direction. It had glowing white eyes.

"I huddled by the door while it searched the bedroom. It was almost like it expected me to be there. As it left, I guess it saw me. The thing got closer, and the shadow got smaller until it finally became John. I tried to act freaked out about John's gun in his hand. I guess it worked. The demon never showed itself to me on purpose."

Jim pointed to Robert, "Can you update us on what has happened to John since he was arrested?"

Robert held up his finger while he finished chewing his sandwich. He finally spoke, "John made bail early this morning. I followed him out of town to the county line. The last I saw him, he was headed for I-40. That means he could either be headed to Nashville or Charlotte."

Jamie turned to Robert, "Why those two places?"

"Human trafficking hotspots. To be honest, this is the first issue we've had with this sort of thing. Most of these guys prefer to travel the interstates and offer up the women at big events or even put them on planes to other countries."

David scowled, "It's like we're back to slavery."

Robert replied, "It is slavery. Today there are more enslaved people in the world than in the 1800s. Worse, they come from all walks of life and locations. You would have difficulty picking them out just walking down the street. Most forced labor immigrants are kept on farms far off the beaten path. Jim and Oliver already had a taste of the sex trade last night."

Oliver leaned around Jaimie, "Wait, he's gone, just like that?"

Robert nodded, "Like I said, he made bail. Although he's a Mexican national, he has lived in the U.S. for some time with a legal immigration status; at least, that is what we were able to find on our systems. Given the lack of any accent, I'd say he's been here for some time. Also, don't ask me how, but he had no outstanding warrants. So, the judge didn't deem him a major flight risk for showing up to court."

David drummed the table, "So much for the exorcism."

Everyone got quiet, and Robert finished his sandwich. Oliver closed his eyes. He could swear someone was behind him. He looked over his shoulder, but nothing was there.

Jim looked in the same direction, "Did you hear something?"

"No, just thought I did. Did you."

Jim shook his head no.

Oliver continued, "I think John will be back."

David stared into Oliver's eyes until he had to look away. David asked, "Why would you say that?"

Oliver looked in Robert's direction, "Am I right in assuming most sex traffickers prefer locations with power and water? I mean, the women bathe at least occasionally, right?"

Robert nodded, "Yea. That's one of the strange things about this case. You wouldn't bring women here unless you plan on renting them to clients or trading them off with someone else. Either way, you want them to be presentable. These women were dirty and malnourished, and most were detoxing off drugs. Normally these guys like to keep the women doped up. It makes them easier to handle."

"Disgusting," said Jaimie.

Oliver continued, "I think this demon brought John here for a reason. Whatever it was, it was important enough for him to ignore his business. If it's that important, he'll be back. When I was with him, John was talking to himself, or maybe it was the demon. I was a problem either way, and he kept saying he couldn't have the attention."

Robert interjected, "Well, he got plenty of attention."

Jim nodded, "Yea. It's possible the demon left John and is at the house."

David spoke, "There's only one way to be sure."

All four of the team said in unison, "We have to go back to the house."

Robert stood up, "Well, call me if you need me."

David gave Robert a wry smile, "You're not coming along?"

Robert padded him on the shoulder, "You have your job, and I have mine. Have a nice day."

Robert walked to his car, and the team made plans to meet at the house that night.

Chapter Six

J im drove down the familiar driveway. David was already there with the back of his SUV open. Judging by the number of cables coming out of the house's front door, he had been placing static cameras on the property.

Jim slid out of the truck cab, "Hey man, you gonna do all the hard work yourself?"

David looked over his shoulder, "I wanted to get this done before it gets dark. Normally I'd say it doesn't make any difference, but there is something about this place. When the sun goes down, it's like you're in a completely different house."

Jim looked up at the sky and checked his watch, "It's only seven-thirty. We have almost an hour and a half of daylight left."

David looked back again, "Where do you want the command center? I think out here is the safest bet. If you remember our last investigation, all the house's rooms were active."

"But we used the kitchen last time."

David stood up from the back of his vehicle and faced Jim, "Yea, and if you'll recall, we had to wait until the next day to get our gear after getting run out of here. I'd like to be able to retrieve our computers before we leave tonight. The cameras can stay if necessary."

Jim looked around, "Okay, where's the table?"

"I thought you had it in the truck."

Jim answered, "Not me. Let me call Oliver."

Jim chatted on the phone and then hung up, "Ollie doesn't have one either, and he'll be here soon. Let's use my tailgate. I have some chairs in the back of the truck. You won't be able to sit in front of the screens, but whoever listens to audio can take a load off and switch positions later."

David nodded his approval. Jim headed to the truck and turned it around as Oliver came down the driveway. Oliver walked toward Jim and David with his EMF reader in hand,

"Hey, guys. Oh, nice. That'll work. Sorry about the table. I thought Jim had it."

Jim crossed his arms.

Oliver looked around, "Where's Jaimie?"

David grunted, "Don't worry, she'll be here."

Jamie's pink jeep turned in at the top of the driveway a few seconds later. She was soon parked, and at the back of her vehicle, Jim smiled at the scene of Oliver skipping towards her. Jim elbowed David.

The two watched as it appeared Jamie and Oliver were in a minor disagreement. A few seconds later, Oliver came around with two cases of gear. His face was red, beads of sweat glistened on his forehead, and his face grimaced. His grunt was unmistakable as he tried to put the gear down gently.

Jamie pointed at Oliver, "See. You better not be hurt. I need you; we need you here tonight."

Oliver groaned as he stood, "Don't worry about me. I'll feel better when the pain goes away."

Jamie continued, "I'm not some weak female. I am more than capable of carrying my own weight."

Oliver blushed, "I know. I was, uh, well, trying to be helpful."

"Try harder."

Jim looked at David and stretched his eyes. David ignored the expression and got back to work. Thirty minutes later, the team had a home base in the driveway, their gear out and ready to go.

Oliver asked, "It's still daylight. Should we go in and get a baseline?"

David answered, "Good idea. Jim and I will go in. You stay out here with Jaimie and monitor the cameras."

Jim interjected, "Wait. Ollie and I normally team up."

David turned his attention to Jim, "Let's shake it up tonight if that's alright with everyone."

Oliver and Jaimie agreed.

Jim shrugged and followed David inside. The fading afternoon sun pierced through the house's dirty windows and dusty rooms.

David turned to Jim, "Why don't you run the EMF, and I'll run the camera. We'll head to the basement first and run with the lights on the camera instead of the night vision."

Jim took a slow breath. It was stale and dank. "One question first. What's up with you and Ollie?"

"What do you mean?"

He turned off the EMF reader, "Don't play coy. You know what I mean. Us teaming up tonight, and why do you care if he and Jaimie like each other?"

"I have my reasons. Besides, they could be a liability."

Jim asked, "How? And why team them up if you're worried about the two of them together?"

The corner of David's mouth turned up. Jim noticed the gleam in his eye. He punched David in the shoulder, "You jerk. You teamed them up because you think their feelings will keep any negativity away."

"As I said, it could be a liability. I'm trying to make sure it becomes an asset. You heard what Oliver said happened in the basement. We can't be too careful. It knows you too. I figured it's safer if we're together if anything comes after you."

Jim turned on his EMF reader, and the two crept into the dark basement. With each step they took, the old steps groaned and creaked.

Jim could hear his breathing and heartbeat. At the bottom, David threw holy water on the satanic symbols. Jim pointed to the bedroom door. David nodded, and the two crept along the wall rather than across the main room.

There were no sounds. The perfect silence only increased Jim's nerves. He had hoped to hear a mouse, a cricket, anything. Everything was dead quiet. The EMF meter remained nominal. David swept the room with the video camera until they reached the bedroom doorway. David was about to take a step, and Jim stuck his arm out to stop David. He placed the EMF reader against the wall. A green dot flickered and then disappeared.

David nodded once. The two stepped into the bedroom. Two green lights at the top of the meter lit up, and a faint tone could be heard. Jim continued further inside, and the readings got stronger. He set the device on the floor, and all the lights lit up, and the meter buzzed.

Jim spoke up, "Okay, we know you're here. Can you step away from the device?"

Nothing changed.

David tried, "We can use this device to communicate with you, but you have to step back from it."

The tone and strength remained unchanged. Jim walked over and waved his hand across the antenna to check if the meter was hung. The tone wavered but returned to its loud buzz when he stepped away.

David lowered his camera, "Pick it up and turn it off. Whatever is here, it doesn't want to chat."

Jim picked it up, turned it off, and dropped it in his front pocket. "Hey David, do these things ever get warm?"

"Not that I'm aware."

Jim pulled the device out of his pocket. The back of the meter was hot to the touch. He opened the battery compartment. The batteries scorched his fingertips. His fingers burned as he fought to pop the batteries onto the floor. After getting the batteries out, Jim returned the meter to his pocket and pointed at the camera.

"Is your device alright?"

David checked his equipment, "Yea, it's fine. Here, take the camera. I want to try something."

Jim aimed the camera at David. David removed a small bottle of holy water and began to spread it around the floor and walls as he recited a prayer.

In a moment, the house seemed to explode. The flooring above shuddered to the very frame. David stopped and turned to Jim. He mouthed, "Whoops."

The smell of sulfur began to fill Jim's nostrils, and he gagged. Every breath he attempted to take made his stomach heave. Jim pointed to the door, and David nodded. They hurried to the stairs. The floor was now wet, and the moldy carpet stank of death. Both men bound up the steps and closed the door to the basement.

They stumbled outside and split apart in opposite directions. Each man did what he could to relieve his stomach and regain his breath.

Jaimie ran over, "What happened?"

Jim gasped, "You didn't hear?"

Jaimie looked over at Oliver and yelled, "Did you hear anything?"

Oliver shook his head.

Jim gagged and spat two more times before joining Jaimie and David, "The whole house shook. It sounded like a bomb went off."

Jaimie answered, "Sorry, we didn't hear a thing. On the monitors, we saw you guys playing with the EMF meter. When David spread the holy water, the signal scrambled, and then we saw you both stumbling to the stairs like you were trying to climb over each other."

David said, "It's a series of old tricks by demons. Sulfur, water on the floor, and the stench of death. It was letting us know he didn't want us there."

Oliver walked over, "So, what? Does that mean we have to call it a night?"

David responded, "Not a chance. We aren't done here."

Chapter Seven

Oliver looked over at Jim. His face was sweaty, and he looked exhausted. David walked away from the team to the command center to check the monitors.

"Jim, are you going to be alright?"

Jim stared at Oliver for a couple of seconds, "Yea. It was just the fumes. It was like someone left raw hamburger baking in the sun for two weeks and covered it with sulfur."

"Do you think it was the demon that I saw?"

Jim moaned and stretched his back, "I don't know. It definitely has some power."

Oliver and the other two stood there looking at the open front door. The dark entryway was quiet. Crickets chirped in the tall grass, and frogs croaked in the woods beyond. Oliver looked up. The stars appearing above in the dusk sky twinkled. The sound of David walking back in their direction caught his attention.

David approached the team with a digital recorder in his hand. He walked up to Oliver, grabbed his right hand, and slapped the recorder into it. Oliver squeezed the device and let out a sigh.

David pointed at Oliver and Jamie, "You two. Go inside and see if you can get that thing in the basement to talk to you."

Oliver put up his hands, "Whoa, are you crazy? You spent all this time saying we could be liabilities, and now you want us to literally go into the devil's den?"

Jim spoke up, "Dave, I have to agree with Ollie. Maybe we should give it a couple of days or get our pastor to come with us."

David shot back, "No. We don't even know if this thing was with John. Just go down there and play nice. See if you can get a name. Negotiate and see if we can investigate the rest of the house. It's obvious that whatever it is, it wants to be left to itself. If this isn't the demon attached to John, I say we leave it alone and see what else we can find."

Oliver responded, "Maybe Jaimie should stay here."

"No, I need her with you. Jaimie, you can tell if it's still in the basement. If it isn't, then both of you come out, and we'll leave."

Jaimie answered, "Ollie, we're a team. We either work as a team or we don't."

Oliver felt his heart begin to race. "No. Of course. Come on."

Jim offered up good luck, and David began to pray. The two entered the front door.

Jaimie whispered, "Do you feel that?"

Oliver responded, "Yea, the air feels heavier, thick."

The two slowly walked to the basement steps with their flashlights on. When they reached the bottom, Jaimie grabbed Oliver's hand. Instead of feeling excited or thrilled, Oliver just felt frightened.

Jaimie whispered, "It's still down here."

Oliver nodded. They both crinkled their noses and moved along the wall to avoid the wet, stinking carpet. As they neared the bedroom door, Jaimie grabbed Oliver's arm, "I can feel him. He's pure hatred and definitely in the bedroom."

Oliver nodded, took a deep breath, and coughed slightly. He stepped inside the room with Jaimie close behind. Both flashlights scanned the empty space. There was no foul odor, but the air was stale and still. Nothing made a sound.

Oliver cleared his throat, "Excuse me. I know you're in here, whoever you are. I'm not here to disrespect you. I won't throw any holy water around. I just want to ask a couple of questions."

Oliver pressed the record button and extended his arm. "I'm here at the request of a friend. Can I have your name?"

Jaimie and Oliver waited a full minute. All was still dead silent, "Do you know who we are?"

Another minute. Oliver longed for the crickets outside, "Are you a friend of John?"

Oliver's hand began to shake. He put the recorder in his left hand. Jaimie reached down and started to rub his right hand, "Who is John?"

Still more silence, but something had changed. Oliver realized the room had been getting steadily warmer. He looked over at Jaimie. She had missed it too. Beads of sweat glistened against her forehead.

She whispered, "What?"

"It's hotter."

Jaimie blinked and then wiped her forehead. Oliver asked, "If you want us to leave, please make a noise."

Three loud knocks hit the wall near the doorway.

Oliver looked over at Jaimie, "Three knocks to mock the trinity."

Oliver turned and scanned the room as he spoke, "My God will not be mocked, but I'm not here for a battle. We won't come down here anymore tonight, but we will be in the rest of the house. If you cause us a problem, we'll cause a problem for you. Do you understand?"

Oliver held his breath. His heart pounded against his chest and in his ears. He waited only a few seconds, but it felt like an eternity. Finally, he said, "I take your silence as a yes."

Turning off the machine, Oliver and Jaimie left the room and headed for the stairs at a brisk pace. Before long, they were in the front yard. The crickets still played, and the frogs still sang. Both grabbed their knees and panted like they had run a marathon.

Oliver heard Jim's voice first, "Are you two alright?"

Oliver stood, took a deep breath, and let it out, "Yea, that was intense."

Jaimie did the same, "I have never felt hatred like that. It was overwhelming."

David took the device, "Well, let's hook it up to the speakers and see what we got."

The group trudged through the tall grass to the command center. David plugged a set of speakers into the earphone jack. He looked at Oliver, "I hope you got something good."

David hit play, and the team huddled around the device. When they got to the name, there was only silence for sixty seconds. When asked if it knew who was in the room, a growling voice replied, "Ollie and Jamie."

Then a creepy laugh sounded as though it echoed through the room. The team stepped back, and Oliver shivered.

When asked if it was a friend of John's, there was another sixty seconds of silence. When asked who John was, a chorus of voices, deep and high, replied, "Everything."

Oliver was about to turn off the recorder, but David stopped him. David listened through the next several seconds of Oliver's negotiating to investigate the house. Immediately after Oliver's last statement, the deep voice yelled, "and stay out!"

The team jumped at the unexpected reply. Everyone stood silent for several seconds. Instinctively Oliver grabbed Jaimie's hand, and she stepped closer to him. The crickets in the yard had stopped chirping, but the frogs still sang in the woods. A gentle breeze blew across the grass and into the forest.

David looked around, "Okay, that wasn't what I expected. I thought this was the demon attached to John. Obviously, it isn't. It could even be more than one based on that last answer. Show of hands, how many want to go in as a team and investigate the upper floors?"

Jim raised his hand first, followed by Oliver and Jaimie in unison.

The corner of David's lip raised up just a little, "Okay. I have to admit, this one even scares me. Let's keep together and stay on the same floor. Jim, you carry the SLS so that we can see if any figures show up. Oliver, let's have you take the spirit box. This way, we can get real-time responses and know if we're in danger. Jaimie, you do your thing. I'll take a couple of meters to set about the property. Command center will take care of itself for this one."

The team grabbed their gear. Jaimie led the way, with David and Oliver behind her and Jim bringing up the rear.

Jaimie stopped at the front door and looked over her shoulder, "Here we go again."

Chapter Eight

Oliver looked back at Jim, "You alright?"

Jim gave a silent nod. He watched the team disappear into the darkness as they entered the front door.

He stepped past the threshold. Stale air filled his lungs, and a heaviness pressed against his body. The SLS camera mapped out the stick figures of his companions in front of him. He scanned the foyer, but there was nobody else there.

Jaime stopped, and the team huddled around her. She whispered, "He knows we're up here."

David took point, and Oliver followed. Jaimie walked between Oliver and Jim. Jim took two steps and then did a three-sixty with the camera. Everyone took a left into the dining room. David began sweeping the room for EMF readings. His devices remained silent. The house's silence was maddening. Jim couldn't find even an insect in the dusty, rotted room.

David pointed to Oliver, "Turn that on. Let's see what we get."

Oliver switched on the device that began sweeping every radio frequency in hopes of catching a voice that traveled across channels. Although the device was a newer model, the white noise sounded almost deafening in the silent home.

Oliver asked, "Who's with us?"

The team stood for several minutes, but nobody answered. He asked again.

This time a deep laugh seemed to emanate through the spirit box and into the walls of the room. The team huddled closer together.

Oliver asked, "Who are you?"

The laughter grew louder. Jim tilted his head, trying to decipher where the sound was coming from.

David spoke loudly, "Turn that thing off."

The laughter stopped when the box shut off.

Oliver looked at Jaimie, "Are you okay?"

Jaimie's voice was shaky, "He's directly below us. It's getting off on our fear. It's not even like he's happy about it. It's more like a twisted hatred that is feeding off torturing our minds."

Jim asked, "Is he coming up here?"

Jaimie cocked her head, "No. I think he's content to do what he's doing."

David spoke, "Alright, I doubt we will get anything worthwhile down here. Let's try upstairs. I'm hoping he'll leave us alone up there."

"I'll take point this time," said Jim.

Jim lowered his SLS camera and walked back out to the entryway. He shined his flashlight on the stairwell. The wooden stairs had long ago lost their stain. The gray, dry-rotted wood was cracked in some spots and broken through in others.

Jim turned to the group, "Take your time."

He carefully placed his feet towards the sides of each step and slowly worked his way up the staircase. The rest of the group spaced themselves until they had made it to the second floor.

Jim shined his light on the upstairs flooring. Although gray and worn, it appeared more solid. Each step caused the flooring to creak.

With the four walking in a line, Jim began to wonder how strong the floor was as it groaned loudly in protest.

Jim began to scan with the SLS, but nothing appeared. The team began to walk by the main bathroom. A stench wafted out of the room, and everyone began to gag. David turned his light into the lavatory.

Jim almost lost the contents of his stomach, as did everyone else. Although there was no water, it was evident that John had the women using the restroom regardless. Everyone hurried forward to the far bedroom. David rushed in front of Jim and stopped him.

David said, "Everyone, this is where we saw the demon that chased us out last time we were here. Remember, this is the master bedroom. If that other bathroom is any indicator, we want to avoid the master washroom. It's on the far side to the left. Let's stay on this side of the room. If this thing is still around, we may get some answers, even if they're lies."

David walked into the room and made a hard right. Judging from the odor, Jim believed David was right about the restroom on the other side of the bedroom. David took a couple of steps forward and put down his EMF reader.

He looked around the room, "We're back. We aren't here to hurt you, but you are not allowed to get near us. Do you see the device on the floor? Touch it if you remember us."

After several seconds nothing happened.

Jim asked, "Do you think it got chased off by these stronger demons?"

David answered, "I doubt it."

Oliver pointed towards the bathroom and whispered, "Look."

Jim looked over and saw a black shadow in the darkness. It appeared to be hovering near the door. He pointed his SLS camera in that direction. A stick figure appeared to be twitching left and right, then up and down.

Jim spoke up, "I can see you. Just come over to the device. You used it before."

The shadow disappeared, and Jim's eyes widened as the stick figure moved closer. The EMF meter began to beep in a few moments, and lights began to blink.

David said, "Good. Now please step back."

The meter was quiet.

David continued, "Alright, I want you to touch the meter for yes, do you understand?"

The meter lit up for a few seconds and went silent.

Jim said, "I can see him clearly now. He's about three feet tall."

David asked, "Are you hiding from the thing downstairs?"

The meter turned on and then off.

Everyone looked at each other. David scanned the room with his flashlight, it appeared empty, but the stick figure remained on Jim's device. "He's still here."

"Let's try the spirit box," suggested Oliver.

Everyone nodded. The device turned on.

Jim exclaimed, "No. He disappeared. No, wait, he's back."

Oliver said, "I know this is loud, but we can hear you with it. Was the demon in the basement always here?"

A shrill voice answered, "No."

Oliver continued, "Do you know its name?"

For several seconds nothing was said.

"Okay," said Oliver, "Is it the same demon that John has?"

The screechy voice replied, "No."

David stepped forward, "Who is John?"

The voice sounded like a shriek through a cavern, "Everything."

Jim asked, "What does that mean?"

The device was silent except for the white noise. A couple of seconds later, Jim saw the stick figure disappear again, but he did not return.

"He's gone from the SLS."

David walked over and grabbed the EMF meter, "Alright, I think we're done. Let's head outside."

Jim retook the rear. He kept scanning behind them like a soldier preparing for a rear attack. They carefully made their way down the stairs and out of the front door. David wrestled the piece of plywood lying on the ground over the entrance, carefully avoiding their wires. Jim drank in the fresh air and the sounds of crickets and frogs again.

Oliver asked, "Who's going back to get the equipment?"

David answered, "Nobody. The basement is far too dangerous tonight.

"Jaimie, can you meet me around eleven tomorrow? We'll get the cameras."

"Sure."

Jim turned off the SLS, "Who knows, maybe we'll catch something after we leave."

David answered, "I'm pretty sure we have what we came to get."

Jim asked, "What about a name?"

Oliver jumped in, "No demon will give you their name the first time you ask. They know we can cast them out as soon as we have it. What are we going to do now, though? John is missing. I'm not sure we want him to come back here. There's a new demon on the property. Why? We don't know. I think we have more questions than answers."

"I'll give Robert a call," offered Jim, "Maybe he can dig deeper into John."

David said, "Well, when you talk to him, tell him time is of the essence. Suppose John is everything? Demons as strong as the one in the basement are beginning to show up. This is something bigger than cleansing a property."

Chapter Nine

S team wafted up from the mug of coffee below Jim's face. He breathed in its fragrance and smiled. The lush green forests clung to the side of the Blue Ridge Mountains. They slowly disappeared into a bluish hue on this hazy morning.

The horrors of the previous night seemed far away. It was hard to believe that just a few miles down the road sat an empty home with darkness that voided the beauty outside its door.

Golden finches flew around one of the bird feeders the apartment complex had put out in the grassy field behind his building. A pair of cardinals sat in a nearby tree, looking for danger before coming to feed.

Jim flipped open his computer and started going through his work emails. The quarterly company meeting was coming up next week in Winston-Salem. He knew he needed to review his team's reports that sat in his inbox for his presentation. The occasional trips to the office could be annoying, but he was looking forward to getting out of town for a week.

The doorbell pulled Jim away from a developer's update he was focusing on. A quick check of the computer's clock showed noon.

Jim jumped up, "Oh, shoot."

Jim hurried to the door and opened it. Robert stood there in uniform with a smile and a folder nestled between his arm and body.

"Please, come in. Do you want anything to drink? Maybe some sweet tea?"

Robert answered, "Don't mind if I do."

Robert walked over and sat down at the dinette table. Jim turned, hurried to the kitchen, and returned with two glasses of tea, "Oh, are you hungry?"

"No thanks. I report to work in an hour. I just had breakfast."

Jim took a big swallow of tea. He had not realized how thirsty he had been after sitting outside, "Well, don't let me hold you up. Tell me what you know."

Robert opened his folder and turned it towards Jim, "Our friend has dual citizenship. He was born in Mexico, but his family moved to the U.S. and became citizens. His extended family still lives in Mexico. Oh, and his real name is Juan Perez. So, he didn't exactly lie about his first name. This may surprise you. He has a family in San Diego, California."

Jim leaned over the folder, "How does this guy end up trading human beings?"

Robert pointed down to the folder, and Jim leaned back, "It appears his extended family had a run-in with the cartel about a decade ago. They owned a coffee plantation that the cartel wanted for marijuana fields. Juan offered to join the cartel if they would spare his family. He was a good employee because they have him handling their sex trafficking in North America now."

"What about his extended family?"

Robert's lips curled down, "We don't know. I'm not sure Juan cares at this point. We have connected him to a village massacre in a nearby mountain town. It appears the folks there decided to stand up to the cartel, and the cartel wanted a message sent to the other villages.

"We also think he has been responsible for several U.S. kidnappings near the border. The girls were between twelve and fifteen."

Jim clenched his fists, "This guy's a maniac."

Robert nodded his head, "Hey, let me ask you a question between us, friend to friend."

Jim answered, "Go ahead."

"Is there any chance this demon you guys say possessed him caused all this havoc? I just want to believe that the Juan that existed before the cartel is in there somewhere."

Jim shrugged, "Beats me. It's possible, but that isn't normally how this sort of thing works. Demons look for vulnerable people. It could be they are weak, cowardly, greedy, or lustful. Just pick a flaw. They weasel their way in inch by inch. If the person welcomes the changes, they eventually take them over."

Robert asked, "What's the end game? The demons have a place to hang out for a few decades?"

"Not exactly. Demons hate us, full stop. According to the Bible and lore, it's because we were formed from dust in the image of God. The lore says that God wanted Satan to serve man, and that is what caused Satan to rebel. The demons and Satan are working around the clock to take as many souls to hell as he can. In addition, they do their best to make life miserable here on earth."

Robert sipped his tea. Jim noticed Robert's face was a little paler.

Robert finally put down his glass and asked, "So, God just lets them rein havoc on us?"

"Not exactly," answered Jim, "God did give him the earth to rule over until the end time as we know it. However, no demon, devil, ghost, or whatever can do anything without God's permission. It's one of the most interesting aspects of the stories in the Bible. The book of Job is the best example of how it all works."

Robert held up his hand, "Hang on, I've read that. Okay. I get it. God allows us to be tested or go through hardship to bring us closer to Him and show us His power."

Jim nodded, "And His love and grace."

Robert asked, "So, what about Juan? Is there any chance you guys can get this demon out so that he'll turn back into the man he was?"

Jim took a long swallow of his drink and answered, "It depends on Juan. Assuming he can live through the exorcism. If they have permission to take the host with them, they'll kill him. Another thing can happen if the host decides he wants to go back to the life he had with the demon. The host can be repossessed, often with more than one demon."

Robert finished his tea, "Man, that's nuts. So, the verses where Jesus says to leave your sin or more demons may return and possess you are real? Have you seen it happen?"

"Yes. We tried to help one man. Long story short, he returned to his addictions to sex and drugs. He began to cheat on his wife once more, hang out in strip clubs, and spend the night in heroin dens. Two months later, we read that he intentionally drove his car into a tree and killed himself.

"Suicide is always demonic. The idea that death solves your problems is the greatest lie of all. So, we really need to find Juan and try to talk to him if he's going to have any sort of chance. If we don't, eventually, the demon will take his life."

Robert said, "Well, I have bad news on that front. The DEA says he was spotted in the mountains outside of Guadalajara."

"What? Just like that? It's been what, a couple of days?"

Robert tapped his fingers, "Yea, that's what happens when you release cartel members. They have a lot of contacts that can help them disappear and relocate in a hurry."

"Is that where his relatives live?"

Robert answered, "No, but it is where the higher-ups live. I don't know what Juan told them, but it must have been a good story. He's still breathing. They have him overseeing some of the marijuana harvests. We're guessing they're keeping him out of the U.S. until the heat is off.

"That likely means Juan won't be visiting our little town anytime soon. I don't guess there's a way to help remove this demon from here?"

Jim shook his head, "Not that I know about."

"That's too bad. Well, I need to head to the precinct."

Jim stood with Robert and walked him to the door. He opened it and then put his arm in front of Robert, "Wait, Oliver said he was sure he was coming back."

Robert shrugged, "Well, Oliver's not the DEA."

Jim said, "I know. I almost forgot I got so caught up in Juan's story. Let me tell you what happened last night."

Robert took a step back, and Jim dropped his arm, "There was another demon at the house. It was not Juan's, but very powerful. The beast made David and me sick to our stomachs. A smaller demon we knew about upstairs was hiding from the beast in the basement. Get this, we asked both demons who John is, and they said everything."

Robert leaned against the opened door, "I've heard people say demons lie all the time."

"They do, but the one upstairs was scared and angry. Telling us John is everything is almost like mocking us with the answer. You know, like he knew we couldn't do anything about John, I mean Juan. Normally, there's a seed of truth in the lie, which makes their lies more deceptive. Oliver is right about Juan if these things are waiting and gathering for him. He will be back."

Robert replied, "Well, I wouldn't look for him anytime soon."

Robert headed out of the opened door.

Jim answered, "I hope you're right. Have a good day, and stay safe."

Robert waved as he headed down the stairs to the parking lot.

Chapter Ten

Oliver sat on a large flat rock. He stared blankly past the swinging bridge across the chasm towards the parking lot. Grandfather Mountain had always been his favorite spot to visit when he needed to escape the cares of his life. The crystal-clear blue sky and the cool breeze could not snap Oliver out of his trance. Jaimie's fingertips wrapped around his forearm.

She leaned in and whispered, "A penny for your thoughts."

Oliver felt a tingle run down his spine, and the hair on the back of his neck stood on end. He instinctively tilted his head to the right and blinked. He turned and looked into Jaimie's eyes. The sounds of other people began to fill his ears. The breeze smelled fresh, and the sky had never seemed so blue for a hazy summer day.

Oliver answered, "Um, well. I wasn't really thinking about anything."

Jaimie teased, "You mean you're here with me, at this beautiful place on this beautiful day, and you can't think about anything?"

Oliver could feel the blood rushing into his cheeks, "That isn't what I mean. I guess I got lost in my own head. You know, with everything that happened and all the information Jim told us on the phone. Why would anyone voluntarily give themselves over to a demon?"

Jaimie moved closer to Oliver and put her arm around him. "Well, this isn't exactly the conversation I had in mind when we left this morning, but I'll bite. From what Jim told us, I think Juan wanted the power. He got caught up in the cartel life and wanted more. He probably thinks the demon's strength is a shortcut up the ladder."

"What about his family in San Diego?"

Jaimie shrugged, "What about them? Nobody knows when he's last seen them. For all we know, his kids could be grown, and his wife divorced and remarried. Maybe he cares about them. Maybe he doesn't. You saw how he treated the girls he was trafficking. Does that look like a family man to you?"

Oliver played with Jaimie's knee, "I get it, but why would God leave somebody like that alive? Why does Juan get to live, but Tracy has to die?"

Jaimie took Oliver's chin and turned it until he was facing her, "Look at me. Tracy is the blessed one. We all claim to believe in heaven and eternal life. Well, Tracy has it. We're the ones who got the short end of the stick. I'm not saying I want to die, I don't, but we should remember life is eternal. It sucks that Tracy is gone, but not for Tracy."

Jaimie let go. Oliver leaned in and gave her a kiss. As their lips met, Oliver no longer felt the hard rock he was sitting on. His head felt light, and the world seemed to spin while her hands grabbed his shoulders, and his muscles tightened. They released their kiss, and the two stared at each other for several seconds.

Oliver finally spoke, "Thanks."

"For what, the kiss?"

Oliver stood up and offered his hand. Jaimie took it and stood. He answered, "For your perspective on Tracy and Juan. Oh, and the kiss."

Jaimie smiled and spoke as she walked past him, "Any time."

Oliver practically skipped behind her as they crossed the swinging bridge. The two shook the rails and tried to make the heavy bridge move from side to side until another couple pleaded with them to stop. The two laughed until they reached the end.

Oliver leaned against the pink jeep while Jaimie attempted to retrieve two water bottles inside the vehicle. The hot asphalt sent waves of heat up Oliver's legs. He looked over at Jaimie, searching through her jeep.

Jaimie looked over her shoulder, "So, do you want to help me with the water, or are you going to stand there admiring my butt?"

Oliver replied, "Do I have a choice?"

He walked over and opened the passenger's side. After a bit of fishing under the seats, he retrieved two warm water bottles.

Oliver held them up, "They're warm, but they're wet."

"Perfect. Bring those to the back."

Oliver met Jaimie at the back of her jeep. She opened the rear and pulled two cold water bottles from her ice chest.

Oliver protested, "Wait, why did I get these?"

Jaimie took the warm bottles, stuck them into the ice, and closed the lid. "For later, silly."

Oliver took the bottle Jaimie offered and shook his head, "A long swallow of ice-cold liquid soothed his parched throat."

Jaimie suggested, "Let's head over to the trees for shade."

The pair left the parking lot and meandered at the edge of the woods. A large tree provided shade, and the two retreated underneath its branches and leaned against its trunk. Both finished half their water before either spoke.

Jaimie asked, "Now that you know who Juan is, do you still think he'll be back?"

Oliver nodded, "You know the whole thing about not wrestling with people but with dark spirits and rulers of this age."

"Of course. It's in the group's mission statement."

Oliver continued, "Yea, well, this is a spiritual thing. That demon we ran into in the basement wasn't there by accident. We know these beings communicate across some sort of network. I have no doubt he knew Juan wasn't there, but he showed up and stayed anyway. Also, that little dark entity upstairs. He was hiding instead of leaving."

Jaimie stepped in front of Oliver, "Do you know what you're saying? You're saying we could have a real evil stronghold coming to our little town. Why? Those things don't mess with places like Hopewell. They go to capitals, big cities, not small towns."

Oliver finished his water, "Look, I don't have the answers. I'm just giving you my theory. I agree it seems impossible. Maybe they're heading somewhere like Charlotte or maybe Raleigh, and our town is a meeting point. I don't know what the deal is, but I know those things are waiting on Juan, and he'll be back."

Jaimie grabbed Oliver's hands, "Then we have to stop it!"

Oliver took a step closer to her, "I'm open to suggestions. You saw what happened to David when he provoked that thing in the basement. Judging from what I saw that night with Juan, the entity in Juan is far more powerful. Not to mention, Juan is not exactly a nice guy. I think the four of us are out of our league on this one."

Jaimie let go of Oliver's hands and began walking in circles under the tree's shadow, "So, what do we do? Maybe get another paranormal group to help us?"

"You know anyone that good?"

Jaimie answered, "No. Maybe one of the celebrity groups. Some of them understand the deal with demons."

Oliver stepped in front of Jaimie to stop her, "You're making me dizzy. David would never allow one of those groups to work with us. In this case, he's probably right. The last thing we need is some non-believer trying to "prove" to television there are demons in the house and escalating the activity. Look, David and Jim will be back next week. We'll see if they've come up with any ideas. In the meantime, why don't we drive down to Boone for dinner."

Jaimie grabbed Oliver's hand, and the two walked in lockstep to her pink jeep. Jaimie hopped in the driver's seat, and Oliver sat on the passenger's side. They descended Grandfather Mountain as the late afternoon sun cast long shadows on the twisted road.

Chapter Eleven

Oliver stood inside a white void. There was no beginning or end. It simply existed. He squeezed his eyes shut. When he opened them, a tall man with broad shoulders stood nearby. He wore an olive trench coat, tan leather pants, and a green shirt with an open drawstring that came to the middle of his chest.

The stranger had brown wavy hair down to his shoulders. His face was shaved, and his jawline was strong. Oliver found himself smiling at the man's face, and although he felt some fear, the joy in the stranger's dark eyes held Oliver in place.

Oliver asked, "Who are you?"

"I am a messenger."

Oliver pursed his lips for a moment and asked, "What is this place?"

"What does it look like to you?"

Oliver's forehead wrinkled, "I remember going to bed. Wait, I'm not dead, am I?"

The messenger laughed, "No, you aren't dead."

"Am I dreaming?"

The stranger rubbed his chin, "Perhaps, but this is more than a dream."

"A vision?"

The messenger began to walk away, "Follow me."

Oliver was unsure how far they walked since the scene around them had never changed. Soon though, something changed inside of Oliver. He felt a dread, embarrassment, and then a desire. Oliver stopped.

The messenger turned around, "Ah, you feel him already."

"Who?"

"Come and see."

Oliver shook his head, "I don't think so."

The man walked back and put his arm around Oliver. The coat the messenger wore wrapped around Oliver's body, "See, I'm protecting you. Nothing can see us or hurt us here. We can feel and see him, but he doesn't know we're watching."

"Who are you talking about?"

The stranger removed his arm, and Oliver gasped. Before him stood a group of people, they almost looked like they were floating around a man in the center. Next to the man was a large being. From their vantage point, Oliver thought it was a sizeable fish.

The two moved closer. Oliver's hands trembled, but something drew him further. A wave of desire washed over him, and Oliver's breath grew shallow. The messenger's hand grabbed Oliver's shoulder.

He looked down at Oliver, "Yes, he is strong. You would be blinded like the rest if I were to remove my protection."

Oliver stared back at the giant fish. It had massive teeth. It said nothing but stood semi-upright with its mouth open. Oliver squinted and leaned forward. The bloodied man standing next to the fish was smiling.

Oliver stepped back, "It's Juan."

The messenger's arm gently pushed Oliver forward again, "Yes, he's speaking for the being."

Oliver stood still. Juan's voice sounded far away and seemed to be nothing more than gibberish. "I don't get it. He's not saying anything."

The messenger raised a finger, "Don't let this fool you. If you could hear what they hear, you would be as lost as the people around him. You feel how the beast touches the lusts of your heart. His words are far more enticing."

Oliver gasped.

Juan stuck his head inside the fish's mouth. Its razor-sharp teeth collapse on his neck. It wriggled its body, and Juan convulsed under its torture. The beast released Juan's head. He emerged with part of his skin missing from his skull. His bloody cheekbone poked out from his hanging flesh. One eyeball rolled around its socket, with most of the orb exposed.

Juan gave a ghoulish smile. He laughed, and the crowd joined in with him. Juan began to praise the fish, but the beast sat there unmoved, blood and flesh dripping from its teeth. Juan dipped his head in the mouth again. This time, when he appeared, the damage was not as severe. He and the others praised the fish once more.

Oliver felt sick to his stomach, "Why are they doing that?"

The messenger stood between Oliver and the group, "That is a stronghold. The beast and Juan blind them."

Oliver answered, "So, that's a demon."

The messenger nodded.

"What's its name?"

The stranger answered, "I'm not allowed to say."

Oliver turned and walked a few steps away from the messenger. He turned back, arms raised, "Then why are you showing me all of this? I can't do anything. I'm not David. I'm not even in Mexico. How am I supposed to stop that monster?"

"Pray."

Oliver began to pace, "Pray? Pray? That's it? Did you see that thing? I don't understand. What could I pray to get rid of that?"

The messenger smiled, "Faith like a mustard seed."

Oliver stopped, "I have faith, but I don't know what to pray. I've never taken on something like that. Can David help me?"

"No, this stronghold can only be broken by you."

Oliver pointed to himself, "Me? What happens if I fail?"

The messenger shrugged, "Then the demon continues as you've seen it. Innocent people will be hurt. Eventually, it will be stopped, but God is giving you a chance."

Oliver shook his head, "I don't understand."

"One more thing."

Oliver rubbed his face in frustration, "One more thing?"

"Yes. If you do this, you will pay a price."

Oliver started waving his arms around as he spoke, "What does that mean? What kind of price? Why does God want me to pay anything?"

The messenger opened his arms, "Only He knows. You are just a man. You cannot break a stronghold like this and expect there not to be a price."

Oliver took a deep breath to calm himself, "Will this help Juan?"

The stranger folded his arms in front of himself, "That is up to Juan."

"What about the people around him?"

The messenger answered, "That decision is theirs to make."

Oliver turned from the messenger and closed his eyes, "I wish I knew what to do."

He turned back, and the messenger was gone. Waves of desire pulsed through his body. He gasped, closed his eyes, and shouted, "Go away."

Oliver opened his eyes and found himself in bed with the sun above the horizon. The same terrible desires still rolled around in his head. Visions of the fish demon and Juan would come to the forefront and fade.

Oliver sat on the edge of his bed and said, "Maybe it's only a nightmare. Just shower, grab some coffee, and sit on the deck."

A half-hour later, Oliver sat on his back deck. He sipped his coffee and tried to relax. He opened his laptop. Oliver stared blankly at the screen for several minutes. He finally closed the lid and stared at the sky.

Oliver looked up further and spoke, "Can't I just say no?"

Nothing changed. Feelings of lust and greed simmered, and his mind was awash with the night's dreams.

"I'll call Jaimie; she'll know what to do."

Oliver got up and grabbed his cell phone. Jaimie's warm smile on her photo removed the frown from Oliver's face. He pressed her number.

"Hello?"

At the sound of Jaimie's voice, Oliver's body tingled, and his breathing got heavier, "Hi, babe. What are you doing this morning?"

Jaimie asked, "Who is this? Ollie, is that you?"

Oliver cleared his throat, "Um, yea. I was calling to see how you're doing and what you plan on wearing today."

"Are you alright? You don't sound like yourself."

Oliver scowled, "What do you mean?"

Jaimie hesitated, "I don't know. Please, don't get mad, but you sound a little creepy."

"Oh, um, I'm sorry. I should probably go."

Jamie answered, "No, wait. Ollie, something is wrong. I can feel it in your voice. What's going on?"

Oliver sat down on his couch, "It's nothing. Just a stupid dream. My head's a little messed up at the moment."

"What kind of dream?"

Oliver could feel his face flushing, "It's going to sound crazy."

Jaimie's voice was soothing, "Please, trust me. I won't tell anyone. Besides, given the things we've seen, it's a long way to crazy town. Now, tell me everything."

Oliver started talking and worked his way back out to the deck. The more he spoke about it, the less he felt the temptations from earlier. When he was finished, the phone was quiet for several seconds.

Jaimie finally spoke, "That isn't crazy. It sounds like a vision, and you talked with an angel."

Oliver stuck his feet up on the guardrail, "I don't know what to do. If it's real, what do I pray for? Oh, and sorry for being so weird earlier. I've never had anything like this happen to me."

Jaimie responded, "It's alright. The Angel said you're going to pay a price. Maybe your lust is part of that. I think we better not see each other alone until this gets figured out."

"We're breaking up?"

Jaimie's voice was urgent, "No, don't be silly. It's just that we could end up doing things we don't want to do at this point in our relation-ship. David's right. Sometimes being an empath can be a liability."

"So, I guess Jim is going to go out with us?"

Jaimie laughed. "Sorry, I just haven't had a chaperone since middle school. I can just imagine how much fun that'll be for Jim."

"Better Jim than David. I wouldn't feel comfortable with anyone else being with us."

Jamie sighed, "Yea, Jim will be less of a buzz kill."

Oliver asked, "So, what else should I do?"

Jaimie answered, "I think you should talk to David. He might have some insight. Who knows, maybe he's had a similar experience."

Oliver dropped his feet off the guardrail, "Is that a good idea? He's so intense. What if he does think I'm crazy? Maybe Jim's a better choice for that too. He knows me better."

Jaimie's voice lilted, "Well, if you want Jim to go out with us until we decide to tie the knot or break up."

Oliver jumped in, "No, that's alright. How do I approach David? I mean, this sounds so crazy on the phone."

"I'll call David. I think if I give him my insight, he'll understand the seriousness of the situation."

Oliver stood, "Oh please, don't make me sound like a creep."

"Don't worry. Why don't you do whatever you normally do? David will call you later."

Oliver walked inside his apartment. "Great. Sorry I'm being so difficult. I do appreciate the help."

"Take care, dear."

"You, too."

Oliver hung up and focused on work for the rest of the morning.

Chapter Twelve

The doorbell rang. Oliver glanced up and returned to the work report he was busy editing. The doorbell rang again, followed immediately by several knocks. Oliver shook his head, slowly rose, and walked to the front door.

He opened the door to find David with a rare smile on his face.

"Come on in."

David followed Oliver inside and dropped a tan satchel on Oliver's kitchen table. He began to remove a small vial of water, another of oil, a cross, and his bible.

Oliver spoke up, "Whoa, hang on a minute. What did Jaimie tell you?"

David stopped and turned to Oliver, "She said an angel came and gave you a vision."

"Yea, so what's with the exorcism tools?"

David pointed to the chair at the front of the table, "Have a seat."

Oliver crossed his arms, "Not until you answer my question."

David gently put his hand on Oliver's back and pushed him towards the table, "They're just precautions."

David picked up the cross, "Give me both your hands."

Oliver rolled his eyes, reached over before David could give more instructions, and took the cross. He turned towards David, placing the cross on his forehead and then over his chest. David reached over, grabbed the vial of oil, and put the sign of the cross on Oliver's forehead.

Oliver put the cross on the table and sat down, "Satisfied?"

David seated himself at the table, "You can't be too careful."

"Dude, it was a dream, a vision. It's not like the other night."

David began sliding his equipment back into his pouch, "I know, but assumptions bring disasters. Did you test the spirit?"

Oliver let out an exasperated breath, "Really? I had gone to sleep. Do you test the spirits when you're asleep?"

David zipped up his bag, "All the time."

"Seriously, you test the spirits if you're dreaming or something."

David nodded.

"I should have known."

David grabbed Oliver's wrist, "You don't realize what you've been picked to do. You've been given a chance to enter the fight. The real fight, beyond what's happening around you. You're going behind the veil."

Oliver pulled his hand away, "I thought the real fight was to save souls."

David scowled, "It is. But what you've been shown is the battle beyond our eyes; it's the core of the battle for souls. Dark spirits blind us, influence us, and deceive us so we can't see the truth of our sins and the gift of the Messiah. You're called to take these beings on directly. So few of us get the chance."

Oliver leaned forward, "I'm not sure it's such a privilege. The angel said there would be a cost if I involved myself."

The corner of David's mouth turned down. "I know. If it were easy, God would tear the veil back for everyone. There's always a cost, and not everyone can bounce back from it."

"Is that why you're so serious?"

David shook his head, "The devil's serious; if we aren't, we can be deceived by our old nature. I'm more serious because I know he knows who I am, and he would love to discredit my witness or worse."

"That's not much different than most believers. I don't get it; what cost would the messenger be talking about?"

David let out a long, slow breath and then answered, "It varies. It could involve you, a loved one, or the victim."

"What happened to you?"

David asked, "Could I have some tea?"

"Oh, I'm sorry. I should be a better host."

Oliver hurried to the kitchen and returned with a tall glass of iced tea. David took a short swallow, seemed to admire the glass, and then drank more until half the tea had vanished. He smacked his lips, "That's some of the best tea I've had in a while."

"Thanks."

David put down the glass, "My encounter was not nearly as dramatic as yours. I was friends with a girl in high school during my freshman year. There was something about her. She was attractive like most girls are to boys that age, but she was shy. Her hair kept her face covered. She never wore anything revealing. I suppose I liked her then because I was a new-ish believer and didn't feel tempted when I was around her.

One thing led to another, and I invited her to church. Within a month, she was a new believer. I was very excited. She was my first convert in a manner of speaking. However, her sadness did not go away. It seemed to get worse. I was getting more concerned, so I asked her to meet me for ice cream at the park.

We started talking, and that's when she confessed that her dad had been molesting her. She felt responsible."

Oliver interrupted, "But she wasn't."

David continued, "Right. We talked until sundown about how it wasn't her fault and how Christ forgives her even if her dad had made her think she was guilty. She made me promise not to tell anyone. I promised, but I didn't feel good about it.

That night, I prayed about what to do. I knew I couldn't let things keep going like they were, but I didn't want to betray her trust. After I laid down and went to sleep, I had a visit from a messenger. He explained a demon of lust blinded the father. I was told to pray it out of the home. Additionally, the angel warned me that there could be a heavy cost depending on the father.

I woke up and didn't hesitate. This was the one way I could help my friend and not betray her trust. As I began to pray, I could see in my mind my friend crying in her room. I got angry and prayed for everything I could think of to remove the demon.

When I was done, I felt exhausted and went to sleep. The next day my friend was not at school. I figured she had a cold or something. That night, I was watching the evening news with my folks. The local news brought up a picture of her dad and stated he had shot himself while parked in his car near an empty field.

I rushed to my room to call my friend. When she answered, she sounded strange, almost like she was relieved but sad at the same time. She told me her dad had come into her room the night before. Instead of sitting on her bed and complying, she told him to leave.

The next part terrified me to the core. According to her, a black mist came out of her father. He staggered and looked around her room like he was lost. He looked at her, and a creepy smile came across his face. The black mist disappeared back inside his body, and his creepy smile turned into a murderous look.

"Suddenly, a bright light appeared at the foot of her bed. Her dad yelled and ran down the hall and out of the door. That was the last she saw of him."

Oliver spoke up, "So, her dad chose his lust, and then the demon took his life."

David nodded, "Essentially."

Oliver asked, "What happened to the girl?"

"Oh, we ended up dating our senior year and then broke up during college. She lives in the Midwest with her husband and kids. Life isn't perfect, but they're very happy together."

Oliver sat quietly for a moment, and David finished his tea. Oliver finally spoke, "So, this really is life and death. Like, the permanent sort of death."

David answered, "Sometimes. I mean, a believer can also be killed, but that's not the end for them."

"So, it is a real war. It's not just a metaphysical thing or some allegory?"

David responded, "This is as real as life gets. I can't imagine what the stakes are with a stronghold, but I doubt it involves just Juan."

"Any ideas on how to pray for something like that?"

David answered, "Not really. Ask God to bring things to your mind. That's what I did. So, you know, there is a precedent for this sort of thing. When Jesus sent His disciples out, there was a demon they couldn't remove. Mark 9:29 says when they brought the person to Jesus, He said that type of demon could only be removed with prayer."

"I thought that verse said prayer and fasting."

David stood, "That's correct. However, much older manuscripts that have been found only say to pray. Most people think fasting was added later, so it's been updated to just prayer. In any case, a prayer at any distance away can be effective."

Oliver stood, "Are you heading out already?"

"Yep. I've done what I came to do. I have some deadlines at work I need to get on top of. I hope this helps you out. Let me know what happens. I feel we'll still be working on this even after the stronghold is knocked down."

Oliver walked David to the door, "Thanks for everything. I hope you're wrong and this resolves our issues with Juan, but it's no telling what'll happen to that house if Juan doesn't return."

David opened the front door and then turned back to Oliver, "Exactly. No matter what happens to Juan, I think we will be dealing with the fallout here. Watch yourself. You may want to back off seeing Jaimie until this is over."

"We're already doing that."

David gave a single nod, "Good. See you later."

Oliver closed the door. A shiver ran through his body. He walked out to the back deck and looked at the sky, "Okay, God. Show me something."

Chapter Thirteen

Jaimie and David sat across from Jim. Jim's freshly cleaned and dusted coffee table held a vegetable tray, and three full glasses of sweet tea sat on cork coasters between them. The mid-afternoon sun radiated through the windows. The apartment's air conditioner struggled to compete against the rare ninety-degree day outside.

Jaimie's blue eyes seemed glued to Jim, and he fidgeted. David did not seem to notice while he scowled into his phone.

Jim cleared his throat, "Jaimie, you're sure Ollie's alright."

Jaimie blinked, "Yea. He's just being affected by this demon; at least, that's what David is saying."

David lowered his phone, "This isn't out of the ordinary. If this is a stronghold demon, they can influence people within a large area. That's why they're called a stronghold. These things not only manipulate people but pull in less powerful demons. Those demons, in turn, can cause havoc among the populace."

Jim asked, "What's stopping the world from blowing up?"

Jaimie answered, "In case you haven't noticed, it is."

Jim nodded and took a swallow of his tea. Jaimie popped a cherry tomato in her mouth, and David returned to his phone. Jim stood up and retrieved his notepad. He dropped it on the breakfast bar and leaned against the wall. "How long will I have to babysit you and Ollie?"

Jaimie shrugged, "No clue."

David looked up from his phone, "Until the feeling wears off. Dagon doesn't have control over Oliver. It's just residue from his vision. Give him a few days."

Jaimie jumped to her feet, "How do you know that?"

David looked up at Jamie, "Relax. Know what?"

"The demon's name. Ollie said the messenger never told him."

David turned his phone around. A picture of a large fish with giant teeth sat inside a Google search. "Because I took Oliver's description and did some research."

Jim grabbed a pen on the counter and started tapping on his tablet. He stopped and tossed it across the bar, "David, why are you so chilled? You're normally way more intense, and why this trust in Ollie? Usually, by this point, you'd be talking about how Ollie is out of his league, and maybe he's got twenty attachments or something else crazy."

David slipped his phone into his pants pocket and looked up at Jim, "Oliver and I had a good talk. I understand what he's going through. Besides, I checked him out. He didn't have any attachments."

Jim rolled his eyes, "Of course you did."

Jaimie pointed to the couch, "Jim, come on, sit down, and try to relax."

Jim sat down on his couch in a huff. He crossed his arms and glared at David.

Jaimie spoke up, "I know you're worried about Ollie. We all are. David is convinced God has called him to fight this demon. I talked to Ollie before David. Trust me, that was more than a dream he experienced."

Jim did his best to penetrate Jaimie's kind, blue eyes. "You guys don't know Ollie like I do. We grew up together."

Jaimie interrupted, "We all went to school together at some point."

Jim uncrossed his arms and leaned towards Jaimie, "Yea, did you know Ollie had a crush on you since middle school?"

Jaimie slowly shook her head no.

"Exactly. Here you are, an empath, and you didn't know Ollie existed. Tracy was the genius who got him to invite you on one of our early ghost hunts that junior year of high school. It was the only way we could get him to talk to you instead of about you."

Jaimie put her head down, "I didn't know."

Jim continued, "We were all kids. Ollie always credited Tracy with being the guy who taught him how to step out and take chances.

"Tracy was the only guy I know who could talk me into ghost-hunting. We did it as a group dare—something stupid at first. There was a haunted barn on this abandoned farm. We went up there with an old cassette recorder and my dad's ohm meter.

"We started goofing around, acting like the guys on TV. Tracy started provoking, saying all sorts of stupid stuff, like telling whatever was there that it was a loser, and that's why they died—dumb stuff. Anyway, we heard a loud bang, and the roof shook. The whole roof. We thought it was going to collapse. We ran out of there laughing and screaming for at least a half-mile."

David smirked, "Amateurs."

Jim replied, "We were kids."

Jaimie crossed her legs and leaned against them, "Tracy was always the crazy one of your little group. I remember him randomly showing up on dates when I first went out with Ollie. I know neither of us told him where we were going. I always wondered if he was jealous or something. Later, I figured out he was doing it to give Ollie a hard time. Anything for a laugh."

Jim answered, "Tracy was the one who got me into programming after I was shot on duty. The doctors said I could take disability based on the mental trauma alone. I didn't want to retire in my late twenties, but I didn't want to be a cop anymore.

"We were all close. Then the cancer hit, and all we could think about was losing him."

David asked, "How has Oliver been since Tracy's death? You know, outside this group, you two are the ones who see him all the time."

Jim answered, "I would say he's been fine, but nobody saw Hollister House coming. I had my moment of doubt in everything I believe, but they passed just as quickly. It never dawned on me Ollie would take his doubts to the extreme."

Jaimie spoke up, "You need to remember that Ollie was with Tracy when he died. Maybe he saw something or didn't see something he was expecting. I wouldn't worry about that now, though. I think this mystery and his vision have now put those questions to the side. Who knows, maybe they answered his doubts."

David said, "Well, we all need to keep an eye on him. I trust him, but he's vulnerable. There's always a price to pay when you battle demons at the level he's been called. I don't want that price to be Ollie's faith."

Jim objected, "He's not under the power of some dark entity."

David's brow creased, "No, that's not what I'm saying. He's going to be under a lot of pressure. All of us need to support him with our time and prayers."

Jaimie and Jim answered in unison, "We are."

David replied, "Good. Jim, I know you're going to play chaperone, and Jaimie, you need to stay keyed into Oliver's feelings. He could think he's fine and then be hit with another wave of lust like on the phone."

Jim spoke up, "I still can't imagine Ollie as a creeper."

Jaimie answered, "It wasn't Ollie. Well, not the Ollie we know."

David said, "Right. It's like the Bible says, all our hearts are filled with darkness. You would be horrified to find out what your dark desires are under the wrong circumstances. So, everybody, stay on guard. We know we have at least one powerful demon at Hollister House and possibly more coming. In addition, Oliver thinks Juan will return at some point. If he does, Dagon will be with him."

Jim looked up at the clock, "Well, I have a meeting to call into in an hour. If anyone hears anything new from Ollie, call the others. David, are you going back out of town anytime soon?"

David and the others stood up. He said, "Normally, yes. However, with what's going on, I think I'll plan to stay in town for the next couple of weeks. I can be anywhere you need me in a few minutes. Just call."

Jaimie and David left, and Jim put away the food and cleaned up the coffee table. He went to the kitchen table and sat in front of his work laptop. He started to log in but reached for his phone instead. He dialed Robert's number.

When Robert's voice came over the receiver, the phone was on its last ring, "Hello, Officer Robert Malone."

"Robert, it's Jim. Did I catch you at a bad time?"

Robert answered, "Nope, just slowing down some speeders. What's up?"

Jim answered, "Can you do me a favor?"

"Depends."

Jim asked, "Can you keep tabs on Juan Perez for me? I know you said the DEA claims he's settled back down in Mexico for now, but something tells me that won't last."

Robert was silent for a moment, and then he asked, "Why would you say that?"

Jim replied, "Look, it's sort of hard to explain. I'm not sure you'd believe it if I told you. Let's say the paranormal world isn't concerned about borders or distance."

Robert answered, "Okay. I'll ask my buddy at the DEA if he'll send me the daily updates he's getting. He knows I'm not going to do anything stupid with them. Besides, this guy is wanted for failure to appear in addition to his other charges."

"Thanks."

Jim hung up the phone and turned on his laptop. A sudden chill passed through his body, and he stood up. He looked around his apartment and listened. His electric clock hummed against the wall, and the air conditioner clicked off. Jim slowly sat down in his chair and logged into work.

Chapter Fourteen

Oliver watched the Unix script he had spent the last three days coding complete successfully. He raised his fists in the air and looked around his empty apartment. A message popped up on his laptop.

"Did it complete? Do I get to keep my weekend?"

Oliver laughed and typed, "Yes, Debbie. We are officially done."

"Oh, good. Well, it's a happy hour down here. I'm heading out."

Oliver replied, "Have a great weekend."

He saved his code to the source system and quickly shut down his laptop. If he hurried, he might be able to catch a night out with Jim and Jaimie. Oliver reached down and tapped Jaimie's number in his contacts. He stood for several seconds, but no sounds came from the earpiece. The phone was on but was not receiving a signal.

Oliver frowned and dropped the phone on the couch. He opened his laptop to message Jaimie, but there was no internet. The low battery warning on the computer beeped. Oliver checked the power cord; it was still plugged into the wall socket. He unplugged both ends and plugged them back in. The laptop screen went black and refused to boot.

Oliver scratched his head and checked his phone. The device refused to turn on. Oliver dropped it, took a step back, and started talking to himself, *"Take it easy. You know technology breaks all the time. Maybe it's some sort of static."*

The light in the kitchen began to blink and then strobe. The kitchen went dark. Oliver clenched his fist. He began to slowly walk towards the front door while facing the kitchen.

Oliver raised his shaky voice, "Who is it? I know you're here. You're trying to manifest or something. I have a generator in the other room that can help. If you want me to get it, knock twice."

Oliver stood there, and the apartment was silent. A light began to shimmer from below the kitchen's breakfast bar. It sparked and cracked and grew. Soon, the large blue ball drifted towards Oliver.

He gasped, "Ball lightning."

He rushed towards the kitchen. The ball moved to the living room. Oliver ignored it and dove for the fire extinguisher underneath the sink. He stood up, but the ball was gone. Behind him, he felt the hair on the back of his neck and head stand up. Oliver turned on his heel. Mere inches from his face, the ball crackled but never touched him. Oliver swallowed hard.

His fingers fumbled with the extinguisher. Sparks shot out and hovered around his head. Oliver dropped the metal cylinder. The heat from the ball caused beads of sweat on Oliver's forehead. It became brighter, and Oliver closed his eyes. The light continued to increase in intensity until it pushed passed his eyelids.

A voice whispered in his ear, "Decide today."

A wind rushed past him, and his world went dark. Oliver opened his eyes. The kitchen light gave off its brownish hue inside the room. Oliver slid down his cabinets and landed next to the extinguisher lying on its side. He lowered his head into his hands and focused on breathing.

He pressed his forehead into his palms and spoke, "Really? Did you think that was necessary? I know you're real. I don't know what to pray."

A thought popped into his head, *Try anything.*

Oliver pleaded, "Show me what you showed me before."

Juan and the strangers appeared in Oliver's mind. However, the messenger was gone, and the focus no longer seemed to be on Juan. Oliver could feel the people's confusion, hurt, and anger. They knew Juan was evil, but they were afraid to speak up. The people were lonely, poor, and desperate for hope from anyone or anything.

Oliver stood up off the kitchen floor and began to pace. The frustration from the strangers seemed to almost burst forth from his chest. He wanted to yell, curse, hit something, anything to stop Juan. He had to help these people.

Oliver looked up at his ceiling, "You must bind up the stronghold. You tell me I am your child adopted through Christ's blood. Well, I'm asking You for something You claim to do. You always hate evil. I don't know how but destroy what this demon has built. He's nothing to You. Open the eyes of those trapped by him. Free them and let them decide on light or darkness. You or the demon. Give them clear minds and strength to follow through, one way or the other."

Oliver beat on his furniture and expressed his frustrations for a few more minutes. Then peace settled inside. His heart no longer thumped in his chest. The apartment was still, and birds sang in the trees beyond his balcony.

The cell phone rang, and Oliver jumped. He laughed and picked up the phone off the sofa.

"This is Oliver. Did I do it?"

Jaimie's familiar voice responded, "Do what?"

Oliver cleared his throat. He could feel his face blushing, "Oh, sorry. I thought you might be somebody else."

Jaimie responded, "Okay. Everything going alright? Are you available tonight?"

Oliver replied, "Oh, yea, of course. Sorry I didn't call earlier. The phone was dead."

Jaimie's voice rose an octave, "Your cell phone died? You never let that happen. Tell me the truth. Are you okay? Is somebody there? Should I call Robert?"

Oliver began to pace, "No, no, nothing like that. Look, I'm not sure what's going on. My electronics died, and this orb that looked like a ball of lightning was floating around the apartment. Anyway, I think it was the messenger. He told me to decide. So, I did. I started praying against the demon. It was wild. I've never had that kind of experience."

Jaimie's voice sounded excited, "What happened? Did you banish it?"

Oliver ran his fingers through his hair, "No. It isn't like that. It's, it's, well, I don't know what's happening. I know I prayed, and now I feel like I'm done, at least with the stronghold. It's silly, but I thought maybe that was the messenger on the phone."

"You think angels use cell phones?"

Oliver chuckled, "I told you it was silly. I don't know. I just thought maybe something would happen. You know, the ground shakes, a bolt of lightning, and a clap of thunder. Something monumental."

Jaimie asked, "How are you feeling? You know, with me talking to you?"

Oliver's brow wrinkled, "What do you mean? I'm happy, of course. You always make me happy. There's something about us that feels like joy shining wherever we go."

"Good, I'll be over in a few minutes."

Oliver shrugged, "Okay. I can pick you up. Hello?"

Oliver hung up and gently tapped his head with the side of his cellphone, "Women, I don't get it."

A few minutes later, Oliver heard a vehicle slide to a stop below his apartment. He peaked out of his window. Jaimie had already cleared her Jeep and was bounding up the stairs. He hurried to the door for fear she might break it. He opened it just in time for her to throw herself against him and wrap her arms around him.

Oliver stumbled backward to avoid dropping them both to the floor. His efforts were aided by the wall that crashed into his back. Oliver sucked in a breath, and the smell of wildflowers made him smile. Before he could say a word, Jaimie's lips were pressed to his. He thought for sure she would cut his lip, and then she released him and took a step back.

Jaimie stood there staring and occasionally cock her head to the left or right.

Oliver finally caught his breath, "Um, thanks for the hello. I'm not sure what I did, but I hope I can do it again sometime."

Jaimie pressed her fingers to his lips, and he quit talking.

After a few moments, Oliver raised his hands and stretched his eyes.

Jaimie turned and walked over to the couch. She sat down and patted the seat next to her. Oliver kept an eye on her as he went back to the front door to shut it. He paused and then went and sat down next to her.

Jaimie smiled and spoke, "It's gone."

Oliver's foot started to tap, "What's gone?"

Jaimie put her hand on his knee, and his foot stopped. She continued, "The lust that the demon was feeding you. I feel your love. Your real love, the pure kind. The lust is still there, but it's being held below your love."

Oliver blushed.

Jaimie grabbed his hand. "Don't be embarrassed. I don't exactly make it easy for you. Of course, a girl must know how to use her wiles to catch the man she wants."

Oliver let out a nervous laugh, "Iced tea?"

"Sure."

Oliver quickly rose to his feet and scurried into the kitchen. He fumbled with the ice cubes, glasses, and pitcher.

Jaimie hollered, "Need any help in there?"

Oliver answered, "Nope."

He popped an ice cube in his mouth and bit down. He grabbed their tea and returned to the living room, "Sorry that took so long."

Jaimie waved him off with a giggle, "I understand."

Oliver put the glass to his forehead. The ice-cold container soothed his heated brow. The two guzzled their drinks until only the ice was left. Oliver got up and took the glass to the kitchen counter. He stood at the edge of the kitchen, looking into Jaimie's blue eyes. He could swear they were bluer than the day before.

He asked, "So, what's for dinner?"

Jaimie stood, "I'm thinking homestyle tonight."

Oliver walked around and grabbed his truck keys, "Momma Ledbetter's it is."

Jaimie held up her hand. "Stop. What about Jim?"

"What about him?"

Jaimie slipped her fingers in between his, "Well, don't you think we should give him a thank you before we fire him? David and Jim put their lives on hold for us."

Oliver kissed the back of her hand, "Where's my mind? Can you call them while we're headed over there? My treat."

Jaimie sat with her head on Oliver's shoulder, chatting with Jim as the two headed into town for a well-deserved home-cook meal.

Oliver said, "I need a vacation."

"Aren't you going to Raleigh soon?"

Oliver stared out of the window at the road, "Yea, maybe I'll take a few days off. Get off the grid and spend time with God."

Jaimie pressed her head into his shoulder, "Just don't leave me alone for too long."

"I won't."

Chapter Fifteen

A licia's auburn hair framed her pale face. Large blue eyes gazed back into Jim's. Linville Falls roared behind her. The mist of the waterfall sparkled amongst the red-hued highlights in her hair. The pale orange sunset competed for Alicia's radiant beauty.

She smiled. Her pearly white teeth radiated from her beaming face. Alicia cocked her head to the left, "Tell me, Officer Crawford, do you miss it?"

Jim looked puzzled, "Miss it?"

"You know, carrying that large weapon."

Jim cleared his throat, "It's just Jim now. Who said I'm not carrying it?"

Alicia's eyes slowly made their way down Jim's body, "Why, where would you hide it? Your bathing suit?"

She leaned in close until her lips were brushing his, "What's it like?"

Jim swallowed hard. His voice spoke barely in a whisper, "What is what like?"

He felt her long French tip fingernails slide up his right leg. She stopped mid-thigh. Her fingers sank into Jim's scar, "Getting shot."

Jim groaned.

Alicia's tongue slid inside his ear. She bit his lobe, "Should I stop?"

Jim stuttered, "N.na.no."

Pain spread across his thigh, and a shiver of pleasure sprang up his spine. He closed his eyes, his forehead wrinkled, and his breathing became shallow.

His doorbell rang.

Jim frowned, "Go away."

The doorbell rang again.

Jim opened his eyes. Alicia was gone. A bluish hue lit the ceiling. He gripped his sheets and turned away from the ceiling towards his Echo screen. Robert's face filled the fisheye lens. Jim kicked violently at the sheet and comforter that entangled him. Semi-free, he reached over and slapped at the screen until he hit the muted mic icon off.

Jim grumbled, "What?"

Robert looked down the apartment complex hallway and back at the camera. His hushed tone was hard to understand. "Sorry, we need to talk,"

Jim rubbed his face, turned to his side, and sat on his elbow, "Now? Is somebody dead?"

Robert tapped at the door, "I'll explain when you let me inside."

Robert took a step back, and Jim noticed his uniform. Jim asked, "Official business?"

"Yes."

Jim let out a sigh and a cough. He regained his voice, "Give me a minute."

Jim muted the screen and shut off the camera. He threw the covers entirely off his body and sat on the bed's edge. Fumbling with the lamp on the nightstand, he lit up his bedroom. After a couple of cheek slaps, Jim slid off the bed. A pain shot through his right thigh, and he tumbled to the floor.

Jim looked down at his old wound. Three red impressions aligned on his surgical scar. He rubbed his leg while he fought his way back to his feet. His sore limb held as he slowly added weight. Jim stepped over to the laundry basket of clean clothes. He dug around until he found a clean t-shirt. Then he slipped off his night clothes and put on a clean pair of khaki shorts.

Exiting the bedroom gave Jim a moment of night blindness in the darkness, and his shoulder bounced off the doorway. Jim grunted and slapped several spots on the wall until the light switch illuminated his apartment. Jim quickly navigated his way across the apartment. He released the three locks and opened the door. Robert rushed past him without saying a word.

Jim closed the door, "Hey, come on in."

Robert walked through the living room, turned on the kitchen light, and started to fill the coffeemaker with water.

Jim raised his hands, "Whoa, hold on a minute. I'm planning on going back to bed. I've only had about four hours of sleep."

Robert poked his head out of the kitchen passthrough, "That's why you're gonna need the coffee."

"From the looks of things, you've had your share already."

Robert raised his voice over the water heating in the coffeemaker, "I've got three hours left on my shift."

Jim walked into his kitchen, "Are you ever not working?"

Robert handed him a mug of coffee, "You remember what it's like. You grab that overtime when you can. I assume you take it black?"

"What?"

"Your coffee, you like it black, right?"

Jim took a sip of the hot, bitter liquid, "Yea, thanks. So, what's going on?"

Robert walked past Jim. "Grab your laptop, and let's sit at the table. I sent you an email for us to go over."

Jim took his laptop off the couch and sat cattycorner to Robert, "I don't get the urgency. I could have read this in a few hours."

He opened the email, and his eyes widened. The image of an older Mexican gentleman lay on a silk rug on the floor. Several men with ak-47s stood semi-circle a few feet back. There was no blood or signs of violence.

Jim's face relaxed, and he leaned back in his chair while sipping his hot coffee, "Who's the stiff?"

"That is the local mayor and backer of Juan's enterprise. He and the corrupt police kept the town in check and looked the other way when Juan needed to recruit someone from town. He died of a massive heart attack a couple of days ago.

"Since then, it seems all hell has broken loose in the little mountain village. I don't suppose David has something to do with this?"

Jim ran his fingers through his tangled hair, shaking his head. He muttered, "Ollie did it. He really did it."

Robert tapped the kitchen table with his fingertips, "What did Ollie do?"

"He broke a demonic stronghold. Well, God did, but He used Ollie."

Robert got up and walked into the kitchen. Jim could hear him getting himself a mug of coffee. He looked closer at the photo. None of the men in the picture was Juan. Jim hollered, "So, is Juan dead?"

Robert walked back into the room, carefully sipping at his brew. He smacked his lips and sat down, "We don't know where Juan is, but the DEA believes he's still alive. They said there's lots of radio chatter. It appears our mystery man is wanted not only in the U.S. but in Mexico."

"I assumed the Mexican Feds were already after Juan."

Robert answered, "No, the cartel is after him. It seems an associate in Charlotte caught wind of what happened here in Hopewell. Juan's job was to get the girls to their man in Charlotte with no detours. Whatever lie Juan spun to the cartel unraveled with that bit of news. Remember Juan's family in San Diego?"

"Sure."

Robert continued, "Well, it appears that was a front for a trafficking house. Some local gang bangers laid down a hail of bullets, killing three people inside: a woman, a teenage girl, and a man in his twenties. The LEOs there believe the woman controlled the flow of girls, the teenager was probably someone she liked and kept at the house, and the man was the muscle. The police are certain the gang hit was simply a business opportunity offered by the cartel. I would guess that's how Juan got his people into the U.S. to traffic. Since they killed his contacts and ensured the police would find the house, Juan has no way to gain an income or seek help. At least not in California."

Jim rubbed his face again, "Wow, this is a lot to take in."

Jim stood and made his way into the kitchen to get some coffee. He stopped for a moment and looked towards the entryway. Robert was not there. Jim poked his head out of the pass-through to find Robert looking at the photos on the laptop.

Jim finished making his coffee and returned to his seat, "I still don't see why you woke me up in the middle of the night."

Robert pushed the laptop away from him, "I think Oliver may have been correct."

Jim scowled as he sipped at his mug. He put it down, "Wait, now that Juan is on the run, you think he's coming back? He has two governments and a very dangerous cartel searching for him. Not to mention, this person in Charlotte must know about Hopewell. Why would Juan risk crossing the border and coming here? Why not head south to Peru or somewhere remote and work to find an island to retire on in some other hemisphere?"

Robert sat back in his chair, "You know that isn't how these guys live. They're all about the moment. I doubt Juan has two pesos to rub together. Besides, something important was going to happen here. Something that caused Juan to risk everything."

Jim stared into Robert's eyes, "Yea, his name was Dagon. That reason is gone if Oliver removed him from Juan's life."

Robert replied, "I disagree. You remember what it was like being a cop. Good and evil play out every day in this job. How many calls did you get where there was something off with a perp, and they had no drugs or alcohol in them or mental illness?"

Jim shrugged, "There were a few. What does that have to do with Juan?"

"Don't you think this stronghold, or whatever it was, would impact the physical world?"

Jim answered, "Of course."

Robert continued, "Well, if you were Juan and your meetup for some demon was supposed to happen in Hopewell, where would you go?"

A gust of wind made the windows rattle. Robert's radio squawked, and both men jumped. The dispatcher's familiar voice came over the radio, "Robert, it's Lewis and his wife again. I don't know what's going on. The neighbors say they hear screaming and yelling."

Robert replied, "Roger, I'll head over there now. Screaming and yelling are normal for the two of them."

Phyllis responded, "Well, the lights are flashing all over the house. At least that's what the neighbors are claiming."

Robert looked Jim in the eyes as he replied, "That's a new one. Alright. Don't call in fire. I'll let you know if there's an electrical problem."

Robert released his mic.

Jim spoke up, "They're next door to Hollister House. You should let me come along, and I think we'll need David."

Robert replied, "Grab your stuff and call him on the way. We need to roll."

Chapter Sixteen

J im held the cross close to his chest and prayed silently while Robert talked on the radio. He finished his conversation with dispatch while an impatient neighbor stood next to his closed window, tapping and pointing. Jim could see the sky's pulsating glow behind Phyllis and Lewis' brick security wall.

Robert asked, "You're sure I shouldn't call for backup?"

Jim answered, "Only if you want to get them killed. David should be here soon."

"Well, I can't sit here waiting in the car. This guy's been banging on the window for the last five minutes. The other neighbors are going to start walking over here soon. If you want to wait for David, I'll head inside."

Jim grabbed his arm, "No, don't. I think this could be an ambush."

"Lewis is no cop killer."

Jim let go of Robert's arm and worked to slip his cross inside his back pocket, "In case you haven't noticed, that's not Lewis causing the light show. I'm not sure what's going on. Demons aren't usually so brazen.

If they came from next door, they're baiting us. If I'm right, that gun won't do you any good. The demons could force you to shoot Lewis or Phyllis.

We can head inside as a team, but keep your wits about you. I'll text David before we open the front door and have him meet us in the house."

Robert responded, "Let's go."

Jim and Robert exited the vehicle. Jim started for the security gate while Robert took time to maneuver around the concerned neighbor. Jim could hear Robert telling the gentleman his friend was an electrician and that he was going to make sure Lewis and his wife were alright.

Jim reached the gate and found it locked. He tried the talk box but only received static. Jim took a step back to see if there was a tree they could climb to get over the wall. A staticky hiss and growl came across the talk box. With a pop and scrape, the gate began to slide open.

Robert walked up, "Hey, how'd you do that?"

Jim whispered, "I think something inside opened it."

Jim felt Robert's hand on his shoulder, "You okay, bud? I thought you guys dealt with this stuff before."

Jim slipped his trembling hands into his pockets and looked at Robert. "Huh? Yes, of course. Like I said in the car, I've never seen one so bold."

Robert dropped his hand, "Okay. I get this is dangerous. We'll run back outside if things get too wild and wait for David."

Jim nodded. The two men walked down the driveway, past a dry fountain, and up the steps of the palatial estate. The lights inside the house continued to blink in various windows. Jim finished his text and reached for the oiled brass knob. He turned it to the right, and the door gently opened. The house went dark.

Robert pulled out his tact light and scanned the foyer. Marble tile reflected the light's beam.

Jim said, "Well, at least they chose the dark. I can work in the dark."

All the lights turned on in the house. Jim scowled as Robert pocketed his flashlight. In unison, the lights turn off for two seconds, back on for two more, and repeated again and again.

Jim scolded the unseen force, "Whoever or whatever you are. We'll turn around and leave now unless you stop playing with the lights. Pick one, on or off."

The lights went off, back on, and remained lit.

Jim looked at Robert, gave a short nod, and said, "I'll go first."

The home was beautiful. Inlaid wood paneling filled a library that doubled as a parlor. Ornate oak chairs and love seats were organized into small groups. The two men turned down the hallway and passed by the large dining room. The table was set for twelve as if dinner guests might arrive unexpectedly.

There was a door closed on the right. Robert pointed and whispered, "Maid's quarters."

Jim stepped back and let Robert quietly open the door. He closed it and turned to Jim, "Looks like she's out tonight. I'll take the point. Let's take the servant's stairs."

The two men turned right just as they entered the kitchen. Jim could only hear their shallow breathing. They finally made their way to the upstairs landing. A long hallway greeted them.

Jim whispered, "We should check every room."

The sound of a door swinging open nearby caused Jim to jump. A man walked out in his gray striped pajamas and motioned to them, "Oh. Do hurry up. I haven't got all night." He walked back inside and closed the door.

Robert yelled, "Lewis, get back here now. Where's Phyllis? Is she okay?"

Lewis yelled, "Hurry up."

Robert mumbled, "I'm going to haul his butt to jail this time."

Jim gripped Robert, "No. Trust me. That isn't Lewis."

Robert frowned, "He looked fine to me."

"Please, it's my turn now."

Jim stepped in front of Robert, and the two men hurried to the bedroom. They opened the door. Jim's eyes grew wide, and he gasped. Robert unholstered his weapon. Lewis had his back against the wall, but his feet were not touching the ground. He was a good three feet in the air.

Lewis cackled, "That's right, Robert, shoot me. You know you've wanted to all these years. You were always an ungrateful brat. Uncle Lewis, indeed. You never took my advice."

With his pistol aimed, Robert stepped forward, "You'd hurt Aunt Phyllis. What kind of a man yells and belittles his wife?"

"A strong man who doesn't put up with impertinence."

Robert shook his head, "No, you're a weak man. Weak and afraid of failure."

Jim stepped around Robert and got between him and Lewis. He turned and swallowed hard at the site of the gun barrel just inches from his face, "Robert, don't listen to him. It isn't Lewis. I know it sounds like Lewis, but does Lewis levitate?"

Robert cocked his head to the right, blinked, and lowered his gun. Jim turned to face Lewis. "You failed. Robert won't murder his friend."

Lewis descended to the floor and snarled at Jim, "Have I? What makes you so smart? By the way, how's Alicia?"

"Who?"

Lewis' cackle caused a shiver down Jim's spine. Lewis's voice changed to a woman's. He said, "Oh, did you bring your large weapon?"

Jim could feel his face flush. He reached into his pocket for a bottle of holy water. Quickly removing it and popping off the lid, he splashed it on Lewis, and Lewis screamed and dropped to the floor.

Looking shaken, Lewis stood back up, "I guess I had that coming. Scorned lover and all of that."

"You're no lover of mine, demon. You only caught me asleep."

Jim slung more water, but Lewis ducked and quickly jumped up on the wall and scurried like a spider to the far corner of the room.

Robert asked, "Where's Phyllis?"

Lewis smiled until all his teeth showed in a macabre expression. He pointed at the ground and gestured to the ceiling. Phyllis' unconscious body levitated until it stopped ten feet above the ground.

Robert asked, "Did you kill her?"

Lewis answered, "Not yet."

Robert replied, "Well, put her down."

Jim yelled, "No, wait."

Phyllis' body dropped ten feet to the carpet below.

Lewis said, "Whoops."

Robert rushed to Phyllis' aid, but Jim shoved him against the wall. He turned and began to walk towards Lewis.

Lewis cackled, "That's right, lover boy, come get ya some."

David's familiar voice shouted behind Jim, "Catch this."

Jim turned and reached out just in time to catch David's large twelve-inch cross. He turned the corner around the bed. Phyllis started to moan. Lewis began to move down towards her, but Jim stood over her, holding up his cross.

"By the power of Christ, I command you to leave this woman alone. You have no authority over her or this house."

Lewis crawled up the wall toward the ceiling and started to make his way to David. David lit a stick of sage, dropped it in an incense container, and started swinging it while speaking in Latin.

Jim continued, "Give it up, demon. We have you cornered. You will be banished."

Lewis screamed, the lights flickered in the room, and the entire house went dark. Jim could hear something move past him. He followed. A shadow covered the moonlight in the window and then went through the glass and was gone.

The lights came back on. Jim made his way back to the bedroom's doorway. Robert was on his microphone calling for EMTs.

Lewis sat next to Phyllis, weeping over her and asking what had happened.

David walked up to Jim before he could interact with anyone. He spoke in low tones, "You know that came from next door."

Jim replied, "Evidently. It was also in my apartment tonight."

David took a step back, "What did it do?"

"Nothing dangerous. A lustful dream, and it poked at my leg wound. I'm doing alright."

David answered, "You have to up your prayer life before bed."

Jim nodded, "I know. I've been skipping it. What with everything going on, work, you know, the usual distractions. Don't worry. After this, I won't forget."

David stepped aside, "Well, let's see if we can figure out why they picked this couple."

Jim followed David back into the bedroom. Lewis was holding Phyllis. She had a carpet burn on her forehead but otherwise appeared unharmed. Robert motioned for Jim and David to follow him. They proceeded down the long hallway and then down the grand staircase that stopped in the formal living room.

The room was tastefully decorated with tan leather furnishings and off-white paint. It was far more inviting than the parlor.

Robert turned to the two men, "Look, there's a long history here. I grew up with Lewis and Phyllis. They were like an Aunt and Uncle to me. Phyllis just explained to me that she had a short affair with one of the staff when I was very young. I don't even remember the guy. Lewis never really forgave her. Well, he said he did, but he never trusted her. I guess that's why they've been fighting ever since.

After tonight's horror show, both are ready to bury the hatchet and reconcile. Personally, I'm not sure what to do. I should take Lewis in on a domestic, but clearly, that wasn't Lewis we saw tonight."

Jim spoke up, "I'm pretty good at writing these sorts of reports. Let me help you with the paperwork once the dust has settled."

David asked, "Where are they going to spend the night?"

Robert shrugged, "I guess here. Phyllis refuses to go to the hospital, but I will have the EMTs look at her. Lewis is still shaken up. I think he'll do anything Phyllis asks."

David shook his head, "No, no, no. They can't stay here. Look, the unforgiveness gave the demon a way into Lewis' soul. I don't know if he was completely possessed, but it was close. He's vulnerable. Even with his forgiveness of Phyllis now, he's weak. They could come back and harass him. He could become psychologically damaged in his fragile state, or worse."

Jim said, "Then let's go next door and end this."

David held up both hands, "Take it easy. I want to talk with Oliver and see if anything has happened to him or Jaimie. We need to come up with a plan before we go marching into Hollister House. If you didn't notice, that's not the demon from the basement or the upstairs. That means there's more now.

The sound of footsteps descending the staircase caught the group's attention. They turned in unison. Lewis stood there. His legs wobbled slightly, but the glare on his face exuded anger.

He pointed at David, "Robert said you can destroy the thing that took control of me."

David walked over and held Lewis' hand, "Robert may exaggerate a little. God can remove the demon that attacked you. I'm merely one of His servants."

Lewis took his hand back, "Then do it."

David replied, "It's a bit more complicated. The entity came from next door, Hollister House. We've become aware of multiple demons in that building. Even if we could remove them all, it would not stop them or others from returning."

Lewis looked at Robert and Jim and then back to David, "I know the owner. Their family has always been a bit unusual. I'll make some phone calls. Maybe I can get that thing torn down."

David's voice became urgent, "Don't get ahead of us. It's not just the house. It's the land. We have to resolve this problem. When we're done, we should burn Hollister House to the ground.

"In the meantime, can you and Phyllis stay somewhere else?"

Lewis frowned, "We have a condo in the Keys, but it's sweltering this time of year. Besides, this is my home. Why should I leave?"

The entire group looked at David. Jim noticed the corner of David's eye twitch. He said, "Lewis, I'm not trying to be unkind, but you're more vulnerable than you realize. These entities will target you and Phyllis. You're literally just feet away from each other. If you want to protect yourself and your wife, head to the Keys. Work out your past. Regardless of the weather, you can make this a getaway that resets your relationship for the rest of your lives."

Lewis began to nod.

Jim asked, "May we have access to your house? We'll put up some cameras to ensure nothing has snuck back into your home. Additionally, this is a great location to set up a home base while we work to remove these creatures."

Lewis scratched at his cheek, "They won't come after you?"

David and Jim smiled. Jim answered, "They don't like having us around. We're more repulsive than attractive to them."

Lewis answered, "I suppose so. Give Phyllis and I a chance to pack our things to leave."

Robert spoke up, "Hang on. We still have an assault case."

David answered, "If you lock him up, it will get worse."

Jim offered, "As I said before, I'll help with the paperwork."

Robert capitulated, "Very well."

Chapter Seventeen

Oliver stretched as he stood outside the old diner on Backstreet. The comfort food left him feeling satiated in the summer sun. He looked across the street at the retired citizens selling their wares in the Farmer's Market and longed for the day he could take life slowly, hour by hour. A family of four barely noticed him as they chatted among themselves and passed around him.

The summer tourist season was in full swing. There would only be a few weekends left when people could travel from the Piedmont of North Carolina to enjoy the cooler temperatures of West Jefferson. Afternoon thunderstorms and the slower mountain life offered a welcomed break from the fast-paced city life. Most of Oliver's friends preferred to leave their hillside hamlet of Hopewell and travel to the coast for a change of scenery, but Oliver never grew tired of the mountains.

He crossed the small road to the market and melted in with the tourists. Oliver ignored the produce since Hopewell had its stands full of locally grown vegetables and fruits that were second to none. When a booth caught his eye, he had almost reached the end of his short journey among the marketers.

It was full of dream catchers and statues that resembled pagan idols one might see in a museum. Crystals framed the tables, with prices attached. Different herbs hung in their tiny plastic bags. Many could be found at the local grocer but not at the vendor's exorbitant costs.

An attractive woman stood within the u-shape table setup. She had thick, shiny black hair. Her dark glistening eyes seemed to dance as she looked in Oliver's direction, and she wore a white sundress that left little to the imagination when she stepped into the sunbeams passing in behind her.

Oliver queried, "This is an interesting setup. May I ask what you do?"

The woman's smile sent a thrill through Oliver, "Oh, a little of this and that. Some friends say I'm a pagan, a witch, whatever. I'm a seeker more than anything. I like to sell my wares to help others along their path."

Oliver pointed to a bag of sage amongst the spices, "You may want to hang on to that. You might need it."

The woman stepped toward Oliver. He wanted to back up, but too many people passed by.

The stranger stuck out her hand, "I'm Melissa. What's your name?"

A breeze passed between them. Melissa smelled like the same wild-flowers as Jaimie, and her breath reminded him of cherry blossoms in the spring.

Oliver extended his hand. Her fingers felt cold, "I'm Oliver."

Melissa held Oliver's hand longer than he liked. The familiar excitement building inside him was something he had recently wrestled. He firmly but politely released himself from her grip.

Oliver asked, "Ever been out of the country?"

Melissa tilted her head, "What a strange question. Nobody has ever asked me that before. No. I prefer to stay in the mountains. I have a store in Asheville, but I enjoy doing these small shows occasionally. You know, get the tourists who don't go to the larger cities.

"I'm curious. Why are you concerned about my sage?"

Oliver crossed his arms. "Well, many faiths believe it can cleanse an area of evil spirits. Based on some of your trinkets, you may want to have some ready."

Melissa giggled, and Oliver clenched his fist to fight from joining her. She reached out and touched his shoulder. Her touch felt light as a feather, and he dropped his arms to his sides.

"Oliver, you're as funny as you are cute. They're just statues and rocks."

Oliver answered, "Sometimes. Well, I need to go. It was nice speaking with you."

Melissa stepped back, "The pleasure was all mine. Who knows, maybe we'll run into each other again."

Oliver shrugged, quickly merged into the line of tourists and headed back into the open spaces. He briskly walked towards Main Street. Groups of people slowed his pace. Oliver stopped at the corner of Main and debated whether to cross the street. He looked over his shoulder at the market and then traveled to the other side behind a group of college kids.

He worked his way up to Blackjack's Pub for a beer. Oliver sat outside enjoying the occasional local who passed through town, looking annoyed at all the heavy traffic. The empty shops nearby testified that Covid had hit this area just like all the mountain communities. Other windows held "Now Hiring" signs and "Closed Early Due to Low Staff." He hoped the throngs of tourists were a sign that the economic growth was not far behind.

A cold breeze blew passed him, and he shivered. Something icy touched his arm. He turned and found Melissa smiling at him.

"Who's watching your booth?"

Melissa replied, "The nice gentleman next to my spot. I need a breather. A girl's got to go to the bathroom sometime."

Oliver turned back to his mostly empty glass of beer, "Don't we all."

Melissa giggled.

Oliver finished his beer and stood, "Well, I hate to be rude, but I have some hiking to do, and I'm sure you don't want to leave your friend with two booths for too long."

Melissa let her arms gently bounce against her sides. "I have a few minutes. I'm curious; you're not afraid of me, are you? After all, a demon hunter should be brave."

Oliver coughed, "Wha, what? What are you talking about?"

She smiled and put her lips near his ear, "I can see things. You fight against evil. Your light almost blinds me."

She stepped back and looked away for a moment.

Oliver pointed up the street, "Well, I'm not sure what you're seeing, but I'm just headed up the road."

Melissa nodded in agreement, "I know you're on vacation. You can't hide forever, though."

"I'm not hiding."

Melissa winked, "Okay. Well, I should probably get back to work. Good hunting."

Oliver couldn't stop staring at her white dress swaying with her body as she sauntered up the street and out of sight. He shook his head and continued up the road. Oliver diverted his path to a couple of shops to get Melissa out of his head. Unsure of where to go next, he sat down on a park bench at the corner of the block.

Oliver reached in and pulled his cell phone out of his pocket. The black screen stared back at him, and he started to turn it on. His finger was on the power button when an older man with a cane groaned and sat down next to him. Oliver slid the phone back into his pocket.

The stranger was dressed in gray slacks and a black polo. His gray wavy hair highlighted his bright blue eyes. The stranger's skin was spotted and pale. Wrinkled flesh hung on arms that appeared to have been filled with muscles decades before.

The man nodded at Oliver, "I hope this seat isn't taken."

Oliver replied, "No, sir."

The man stuck out his hand, "Sir, well, somebody was raised right. I'm Lucius. What's your name?"

"Oliver."

The two shook hands. Lucius continued, "Glad to know you, Oliver. You're from around here, or are you just visiting like these city folks?"

Oliver took his eyes off Lucius and watched the people meandering the street, "I'm not from this town. I live further west, in Hopewell."

Lucius nodded, "Yea, I've heard of it. Nice little place. Better than here. These city folks keep buying up land and building. They are trying to get away from their concrete jungle, but now they're building a new one in our town. I bet half these tourists don't remember when four-twenty-one was a two-lane road. Between them and the college kids, there won't be anything left of the mountains in ten years."

Oliver turned to the stranger, "Well, I guess that's progress? I mean, we all need to live somewhere, right?"

Lucius replied, "I reckon so. So, why does a man from the mountains come to a mountain town full of tourists?"

Oliver stretched out his legs, "It's a vacation. I work in computers and had to travel down to Raleigh for a class and decided to take a couple of days off and enjoy the mountains like the tourist do. After all, everyone comes here to relax. Why don't we take advantage of our surroundings too?"

Lucius tapped at the cane and spoke, "For a young man, you have a lot of wisdom. I never took the time to look around and appreciate my surroundings until I quit working. I was always chasing the dollar to keep the kids fed, the wife happy, and my dog faithful."

"What did you used to do?"

Lucius looked up at the sky, "Well, I've done quite a bit, but I guess most folks would say I've been a messenger most of my life."

Oliver's eyes grew wide, "A messenger?"

Lucius looked back down at Oliver, "Yep. Your faithful postal worker, at your service."

Oliver coughed for a moment to stifle his laughter. "Sorry, I just got choked."

"Well, that can happen. I've gotten choked up over a lot of things in my life. Although, I can't reckon meeting the mailman to be one of them. What do you do with computers, if you don't mind me asking?"

Oliver replied, "I'm a software developer."

Lucius cocked his head to the left, "Do anything else?"

Oliver's brow creased, "Um, I'm not sure what you mean. That job keeps me busy."

"Any hobbies?"

Oliver pressed his lips together and then said, "Nothing interesting."

Lucius' lips curled up, "All right. I reckon I've pried enough. You know, some folks say I'm pretty old, but compared to others, I ain't that young. So, if you don't mind, I'd like to give you a piece of advice."

Oliver sat up straighter, "Sure."

"If you're up here to enjoy the mountains, you need to be in them. Most tourists think our small little town is country, but you and me know better. If you're really looking to rejuvenate, you need to head up yonder out of town."

Oliver answered, "Well, I'm staying in a cabin in Fleetwood."

Lucius slapped his thigh and then started rubbing it, "Good. Stay up there. I mean, if you need to eat, come on into town. Just avoid being around folks. You can't really hear what you need to hear amongst all the people and noise. Besides, you never know whom you'll bump into. You might get yourself in trouble without even trying."

Oliver nodded, "That's good advice. Hey, I don't mean to be too forward, but would you mind if I call you next time I'm in town? I'd like to get to know you better."

Lucius groaned, stood up, and leaned against his cane, "I don't see why not. A man can never have too many friends. I'll introduce you to the wife. She can make a powerful good meal."

Oliver stood and grabbed Lucius' hand, "Thanks for the talk."

Lucius nodded once and slowly made his way between a group of people. Oliver turned to walk to his car and stopped. He needed Lucius' phone number. He turned back and found the street empty. Lucius was nowhere to be seen. He walked half a block, but the older man had somehow disappeared. Oliver turned back and decided it was time to leave town.

Chapter Eighteen

J im stood outside Hollister House in the mid-morning sun. The late summer breeze held a touch of fall. It would not be long before the morning would be getting colder again. Jim looked down at the basement door. Although it had been locked, it sat cracked open.

The sound of David's vehicle caught his attention. David's SUV stopped, and he exited with a small tool bag in hand.

Jim raised his voice, "What, no crucifix this morning?"

David put his finger to his lips and walked over to Jim, "I think they're pretty familiar with us already. I sent Jaimie over to Lewis and Phyllis' place to make sure nothing was disturbed. She'll squawk at us on the radio if there's a problem. Well, let's head inside."

Jim put out his arm, "Wait. The door down there is cracked open. Don't you think we should check the outside of the building first?"

David answered, "You're the expert. I didn't ask on the phone. I assume you brought your gun."

"I have it."

David gazed down at the basement, "Good. We may need it since Robert took a couple of days off to go fishing."

Jim took two steps backward, "Follow me."

The two men slowly walked to the back of the house. Tall grass, overgrown shrubs, and scrap metal made for slow going. Jim would stop every ten feet or so to listen. David kept checking behind them, and both men kept gazing at the windows.

On the far side of the large structure, the trees had taken over most of the property to the side of the house. The two men force their way through nettles, small branches, and slick leaves covering the ground. Shadows danced among the windows, but their source was simply the forest. The two men finally broke through to the front yard.

As they slowly walked across the overgrown grass, both men stopped at the front door. Although the plywood appeared undisturbed, all the main cables had been severed and drugged out to the front porch. Jim's shoulders sank, and David let out a heavy sigh.

Jim said, "That's gonna take a couple of hours to fix."

David answered, "Yea. Probably vagrants. At least they didn't steal the cable for the metal inside."

Jim asked, "Any chance this could be supernatural?"

"You ever known of a ghost or demon who could cut cables and drag them several feet?"

Jim answered, "No. Before we get started, we should sweep the house. You were here last. Is it still safe during the day?"

"Yea. You can feel the oppression, but as long as we keep to our work, we should be alright."

Jim said, "We'll start in the basement and work our way up."

David whispered at the top of the steps, "Wait a minute." He pulled the small walkie-talkie from his belt clip. He spoke in a hushed voice, "David for Jaimie."

"Go for Jaimie."

"Someone's been here. So, we're going to sweep the house. Unfortunately, the cables were tampered with. It'll take us two or three hours to fix. You can take off after you finish over there."

Jaimie's voice returned, "Roger. I found new footprints in the mud, but nothing is disturbed. I'm guessing the security cameras over here scared them off. I'm downloading the video files from the system now. I'll keep an eye on the live feed. If I see anything, I'll let you know. You two be careful."

"Roger."

David clipped back the device to his belt, "All right, ready when you are."

Jim slipped his revolver from its waistband holster. The two men slowly walked down the stairs. The door groaned in protest as Jim slowly opened it and stepped inside. Both men waited for their eyes to adjust.

David whispered, "Do you feel that."

Jim nodded and answered in a hushed tone, "Yea, it's worse. The air's so heavy; it's tough to breathe. Still think it's safe?"

David responded, "We know where the exit is if we need it."

The two men stepped further inside the familiar basement after Jim jammed the cable under the door to keep it open. Neither spoke as they walked the parameter of the basement. Jim's muscles would tighten at the sound of a creak or pop in the old house's structure.

David's radio suddenly squawked, and both men jumped. David wrestled with the volume and turned it down.

Jaimie's staticky voice came through, "There's movement upstairs."

David wrestled the radio from his belt, and Jim kept sweeping the area around them. David whispered, "What kind of movement?"

Jaimie answered, "I'm pretty sure it's a man. Too solid to be anything else. Sorry, only one camera is still working up there. I caught a glimpse of someone. I wish I had more."

David answered, "Okay, going silent. Stay where you are in case we need help."

"Roger."

The men heard footsteps walking on the floor near the foyer above. Jim pointed at his ear, pointed up, and then with two fingers, pointed toward the basement stairs. David nodded, and the two quietly made their way to the foot of the stairs.

Jim motioned for David to move down the wall. After David got himself in position, Jim threw his body against the beam at the bottom. A loud thud reverberated in the structure directly above them, and dust fell on Jim.

He took a step back and waited. The footsteps above hurried towards the basement door within a few seconds. The door opened, and a stranger's voice hollered, "Juan, is that you? It's me, Carl."

Jim said nothing.

Carl continued, "Come on, man, don't be like this. You know I had to tell Julio what happened. There are too many eyes up here. Besides, Al picked up three of your girls two nights ago. They were hooking down in Raleigh. They told him everything. At least I tried to put a positive spin on things."

Jim coughed.

Carl said, "Hey, look, I'm coming down. I saw the two cars out front. Tell whoever is with you not to shoot."

Jim grunted.

Heavy footsteps slowly made their way downward. Jim slipped back against the wall and motioned down further away. He trained his gun on the final step into the basement. A small caliber revolver stuck out in front of Carl as he stepped into view.

Jim hollered, "Freeze. Drop your weapon, now."

Carl stammered.

Jim hollered louder, "I said now."

Carl tossed the gun on the floor and stepped into the room.

"Hands against the wall."

Carl faced the wall. Jim frisked Carl and found a switchblade but no other weapons. After relieving him of his knife, he told him to sit on the step. Carl looked up bewildered at Jim, and David appeared from the shadows.

Carl said, "Wait a minute. You're a cop, but that guy, he's no cop, no way. What's going on? You working for Juan?"

Jim smiled and hovered over Carl, "You're right. I'm a cop, well, I used to be. We're looking for Juan, not working for him. Do you happen to know where he might be?"

Carl shrugged, "I ain't talking to no pig, former or otherwise."

David spoke up, "Maybe Juan told you to meet him here? Hey Jim, why don't we tie him up, wait outside, and see if Juan shows up."

Carl's voice went up an octave, "You mean like bait?"

Jim pushed himself off the wall, "I like the way you think."

Carl's hands waved in protest. "No, no way. Look, all I know is that the cartel has a bounty on his head. His girls said he had been in an old abandoned mansion in this town. It's not like many of these are sitting around up here. I thought I'd try my luck if he returned for some reason."

Jim stared into Carl's eyes, "You have no idea why he came to Hopewell?"

Carl shook his head, "Like I said, just trying my luck. Look, let me go, and I'll leave town. If you can get the drop on me in this place, I'm sure Juan can."

Jim tapped his gun against the side of his leg. "You know, part of me would like to let you leave, but you traffic human beings."

"You can't prove that. All you have me on is trespassing. That's like a ticket, and don't come back. Well, I won't come back, and I'll spare your friends the paperwork."

Jim looked at David, "Grab some rope."

Carl's stressed voice hollered, "Wait, what?"

Jim answered, "Relax. I will tie your hands around your back and take you outside while my friend fixes the damage you caused to our cameras."

"Then you'll let me go?"

Jim answered, "We'll see."

After they tied his hands, Jim led Carl outside. The two men sat on the steps while David worked to reconnect the cables. Nobody spoke, and Jim kept a keen eye on Carl while listening and watching their surroundings.

While they worked and waited, Jaimie's pink jeep drove into the driveway. She saw the men on the porch and promptly backed out and left.

Carl asked, "Who's that?"

Jim answered, "Probably a lost tourist or some realtor looking to put the property on the market."

When David had finished, Jim stood Carl to his feet. He began to untie his bonds, "Okay, here's the deal. You're going to walk away from here and not come back. Go to wherever you parked your car and head back to Raleigh. If I see you in our town again, I'll have the cops pick you up."

"What about my gun?"

Jim pulled the gun out of his front pocket. He retrieved the magazine from the other pocket. Carl held out his hand, and Jim handed him the magazine. Then he dismantled the small weapon, took the firing pin, slid that back into his pocket, and poured the pieces of the weapon into Carl's palms.

Carl dumped the contents on the ground, "That's junk without the firing pin."

Jim shrugged, "Suit yourself. You could've bought a new pin."

Carl offered up his middle finger and stomped off towards the road. Jim and David stood there watching him until he turned the corner and disappeared. They continued watching the entrance of the driveway for several more minutes.

Jim finally said, "Hey man, please get the rag out of the back of my truck and pick up those pieces. I'll take them to the station."

"What for?"

Jim answered, "Who knows? Maybe their detectives can link it to a crime. Carl may be slippery in Raleigh, but he sure is clumsy in Hopewell."

David trotted towards the pickup, returned, eagerly picked up the pieces, and handed the bundle to Jim. Jim looked down at his quarry and said, "I hope Oliver stays off the grid and away from here for more than a few days. If the cartel's men think Juan's in Hopewell, they might be right."

Chapter Nineteen

Thunder shook the walls of the cabin. A blue flash lit up the family room, and a thunderclap rattled the windows. A roar echoed down through the valley. Oliver tried to get the weather channel, but the satellite television was hopelessly blocked. The lights flickered with the storm's bombardment, and the television cut off.

Oliver picked up the landline that was still available in the home for an emergency. He felt a tingle run through his hand and dropped the receiver as a blue streak struck a nearby tree outside a window. Bark splintered, and wooden shrapnel exploded in all directions. He grabbed his cell phone off the table and sat on the floor.

It took his Samsung forever to boot up. Oliver went straight for the weather app. It hung but then opened—another flash of lightning. The app hung again. Oliver looked. The cell signal was gone. He tossed the phone to the floor and asked God to protect him.

The wind picked up, the cabin shook, and the roof groaned. Outside the windows, the sky was as dark as midnight, except for the blue lightning strobes.

Oliver whispered to himself, "It's 11 am. I've never seen such a violent storm, especially in the morning. It must be an incredible storm front."

Feeling a bit calmer, Oliver stood and made his way to the bedroom to start packing. He was supposed to leave tomorrow morning, but he might as well make good use of his time. Thunder shook the pictures on the walls, and Oliver instinctively ducked.

He heard his text alert go off. Oliver hurried back to check his phone.

A message from Jaimie read, "Call me, it's important."

The cell signal only had one bar. Oliver tried his luck. After one ring, Jaimie's voice crackled on the other end, "Sorry, we need you back tonight at Hollister House."

Oliver answered, "I don't know if I can. We have a major storm."

Oliver's phone crackled, and Jaimie's voice changed pitches and faded in and out, "Please...Juan...David needs you."

Oliver started walking towards the bedroom, "Okay, I'll find a way."

There was silence on the other end.

"Hello, Jaimie. Are you there?"

Oliver's phone buzzed and began to feel warm. The screen went black. Lightening hit nearby, and the outlets shot out a blue flame. He heard the surge protectors popping all over the house. Oliver tried in vain to find a signal on his phone. He lifted it over his head and aimed it at the floor but stopped himself.

A black screen stared back at Oliver. He stuck the device in his pocket and headed to the bedroom to finish packing. Oliver cringed at the storm, shaking the house around him. He stopped for a moment and looked to the ceiling, "Why isn't Robert taking care of Juan?"

Oliver looked back down and continued packing. He had just finished closing his suitcase when the lights went out. Stumbling down the hall, pulling his luggage behind, he made his way to the front door. He stopped and turned in the direction of the landline in the dark room. With another clap of thunder, he turned back and opened the door.

The dark skies only released sprinkles of water. A gust of wind fought Oliver as he closed the door. He threw the suitcase into the passenger side of his pickup and rushed to the driver's side. Driving down the winding, narrow road, the skies opened up. Oliver turned on his lights, rain lights, and his wipers. He leaned over the steering wheel, attempting to see the road.

It felt like an eternity to get to the four-lane highway. Once he turned on to two-twenty-one, Oliver could make out the road a little better. At least he could sit back and see the white lines on the blacktop through the sheets of rain. A gust of wind pushed against the side of the truck, and Oliver's knuckles whitened against the steering wheel.

He complained, "This is going to take all day."

Oliver turned on the radio. The emergency broadcast system did not take long to interrupt the country music station. An unexpected cold trough had formed over the blue ridge mountains. It created a line of powerful thunderstorms, and the recording advised of possible flash flooding.

Oliver sighed. The safest route was through Blowing Rock, down three-twenty-one, west on interstate forty through Asheville, and then taking the slower highway 74 west exit. Even in good weather, it was a long day's ride.

By the time Oliver reached Asheville, the buffeting storm had turned into a steady rain. His arms and hands ached, and his back was twitching. Pulling off the road was a necessary option. A Starbucks sign ahead promised caffeine and recharge.

Once he got his coffee, he settled down in a quiet corner of the store and let himself relax. While sitting there, he fiddled with his phone to see if he could power it up. A familiar voice broke his concentration.

"Well, I didn't expect to see you again. Maybe we are meant to be together."

Oliver looked up. Melissa was wearing blue jeans and a black shirt. Her eyes sparkled and danced as she lingered her stare and sat in the chair across from Oliver.

"Don't tell me you came to Asheville to find me."

Oliver put down his phone, "Unfortunately, no. This weather rocked my cabin up in the mountains. I decided maybe it was time to go home. I'm just stopping here for a coffee before I finish my drive."

Melissa reached over and grabbed Oliver's hands before he had a chance to move, "Ah, the fates. How kind they can be."

Oliver gently slid his hands free and put them on his lap, "Perhaps, someday. I think today it's more about us liking coffee."

Melissa smiled, tilted her head back and forth, and studied Oliver. He sipped at his warm brew and tried not to show how uncomfortable she was making him. Her mouth began to turn downward.

Melissa leaned in close to Oliver and spoke quietly, "You're not going home. You're going after them."

"Them, who?"

Melissa's brow creased, "The demons. Yes, I can see inside your light. Be careful. It's a trap."

"How can you be so sure?"

Melissa pointed outside, "Nature speaks to us, to me. Storms are not always what they seem."

Oliver replied, "Well, this one was a cold trough, plain and simple. I appreciate your concern for me, but you know who it is I believe and follow."

Melissa nodded.

"Then you know I know what I'm doing."

Melissa reached out and grabbed his hand and coffee mug, "Don't put so much trust in what you know. None of us understands the spiritual realm."

Oliver took his other hand and put it on top of Melissa, "I know, but I have a savior who does. He could be yours too. Who knows what secrets His Holy Spirit would show you?"

Melissa pulled her hand back, "I know, but I'm not ready. There is so much I want to find out for myself first."

Oliver stood, "Well, I'll give you the same advice you gave me. Be careful. Eventually, you can't mess with that stuff and not get yourself in trouble. As you said, don't put your trust in what you know."

Melissa stood up, hugged Oliver, and stepped back, "I know you love someone else, and I'm not your type, at least not now. Do me a favor."

"Maybe."

"Stay alive for her."

Oliver answered, "Well, I don't think that's my decision, but I'll do my best."

Melissa reached over, kissed his cheek, and then turned and walked out. Oliver took his time throwing away the trash before meandering towards the parking lot. Melissa was nowhere in sight. He slid back inside his truck and headed towards Hopewell.

At almost ten pm, Oliver slowly rolled down the street leading to Hollister House. He glanced at the home next door. Pale lights glowed from the upstairs windows. That seemed unusual to Oliver since an older couple lived there. He turned down the driveway for Hollister House and stopped.

Oliver didn't move. He flipped on the truck's high beams and offroad lights. There were no signs of anyone. He began to back out of the driveway but decided to do a quick check outside. He left his truck running, grabbed his holy water and crucifix from his glove box, and stood outside the car.

He spoke in hushed tones, "David, Jaimie, Jim. You guys here?"

****

Jaimie sat staring at the computer monitor inside Lewis and Phyllis' house. Her cell phone lay in front of her.

"David, I'm looking through the footage, and I don't see anything before the screen goes blank. I checked the cables outside the house before the storm came in, and they looked fine. Do you want me to go back and see if anyone is there?"

David replied, "No, it could be dangerous, especially after that storm. The spirits over there will be charged up. I'm not getting anything on my motion detector now. Tell you what. Do you mind checking the other cameras while you're there, in case someone was in the house?"

Jaimie responded, "No problem. Ollie is coming home tomorrow, and I need something to keep me busy."

****

Oliver raised his voice, "Is anybody here?"

A dark figure stuck his head out of the basement door. David's voice responded, "Over here. Cut off your truck and get in here. I need your help."

Oliver took a step forward, "Where are the vehicles and everybody else?"

"Next door. Look, see the cables?"

Oliver looked at the ground illuminated by the truck's lights. Dark thick cables came up from the basement and curved in the neighbor's direction with the lights on.

Oliver said, "I see them. What's going on?"

David's voice responded, "Look, we had some things happen while you were gone. I'm sure I know why these demons are coming here, but I need your help. I think I know a demon's name. I'm going to get it to manifest."

Oliver answered, "Sounds dangerous, one second."

He ran over and turned off his truck and its lights. He trotted back to the stairs, but David was nowhere to be seen. Light from inside cast a pale-yellow beam in the doorway. Oliver eased his way down the stairs.

"Hello?"

There was no answer. Oliver stepped inside and headed towards the light. He walked into the central room of the basement and turned towards the stairs. Nausea overtook his body. Oliver staggered backward, fell to his knees, and began to throw up. A white flash of pain crossed his vision, and everything went black.

Chapter Twenty

Oliver opened his eyes. He jerked his arms. Pain seared the base of his hands. He looked down and found his arms tied down to the armrests with woven cords around his wrists. The horror that had frightened him sat front and center. A stranger hung on the wall. His skin was cut open and pulled apart like macabre wings holding him up.

Juan's familiar voice spoke from behind him, "Do you like it? I'm a big fan of "Silence of the Lambs." Hannibal's character had such an artistic flair. I know that's a poor representation, but I've never been much of an artist. I suppose I wouldn't have ended up like this if I was."

Juan laughed at his monologue, walked around, and stood in front of Oliver. He was sharpening a small, bloodied knife against a stone. Juan checked Oliver's restraints and nodded his head in approval.

A red-hot pain cut into Oliver's left arm. He looked down just in time to see Juan pulling the knife away from his forearm. Juan smiled, "Good, nice, and sharp."

Oliver's breath began to speed up and become shallow. Juan walked over and got in his face, "Don't try and pass out on me. I'll wake you up, and you won't like how I do it."

Oliver sucked in a long slow breath and exhaled. He turned towards Juan, who was at a table to the side, looking at the holy water and crucifix. "Why are you doing this? Who is that?"

Juan rushed over to his side, "Why! Why? You know why. You took the only thing from me that gave me power over others. I don't know how you did it, but you did. I wouldn't have figured it out, except the demons here told me when I arrived. They've been spending some time around you and your friends. You should learn to keep your mouths shut.

"As for our friend on the wall, he's a snitch. His name used to be Carl. I'm afraid stitches aren't going to do him any good except for his funeral."

Oliver replied, "Demons lie."

His head jerked to the left, and Oliver heard his jaw crack. The taste of blood trickled over his tongue, and a warm liquid trickled over his chin. Oliver attempted to move his jaw. It hurt but was still mobile.

Juan poked a finger in his face, "Say one more derogatory thing about my friends, and they'll be feeding you with a tube."

"They aren't your friends."

Juan lifted his hand but then slowly lowered it, "What would you know?"

Oliver answered, "They want your soul. You know, I saw Dagon when he was with you. You were sticking your head in the demon's mouth, and every time you pulled it out, part of your flesh was missing. You were like food to him."

"How did you cast him out?"

Oliver's arm burned. He turned it a bit and answered, "I didn't do anything. God did it. I only prayed."

"Prayed, huh?"

Oliver nodded.

Juan reached out and cut Oliver's other arm. Oliver whimpered.

"It's okay to cry. It's going to hurt. I should know. It happened to me once."

Juan lifted a sleeve. Several scars ran the length of his arm, "I cried most of the time. I thought for sure I'd die."

Oliver replied, "I don't understand. Why do this to me? Nobody knew about your demon but us. Torturing me won't send a message to anyone."

Juan walked back over to the table and picked up the holy water. He returned to Oliver. "Oh, but it does. You see, my new friends want to be sure neither you nor your friends interfere with our plans. Sadly, they wouldn't let me just kill all of you. I suppose someone has to spread the bad news."

Oliver looked into Juan's eyes. "What are your new friends' names?"

Juan's eyes went completely black, and a chorus of deep and screeching voices replied, "Legion."

Oliver quipped, "Legion. Can't you guys update that to battalion, squad, or something newer?"

Juan's mouth twisted into a grotesque smile, "Humans think they're so clever. We'll soon see about that."

Juan's eyes and his voice returned to normal, "I guess my friends wanted to say hello."

"You know, you're not the first to be loaded up with demons. There's a guy in the Bible that was full of them. They eventually drove him insane. He ran around naked in a graveyard. He did have superhuman strength, but he was useless. Jesus cast out the demons, and the man ended up following Him. Maybe you should think about that."

Juan popped the top off the holy water, "That man wasn't me."

He drank down the holy water, groaned, and doubled over. Gagging, he released his stomach contents at Oliver's feet. A scream filled the room, and black smoke expelled from Juan's mouth and evaporated into thin air.

Juan stood upright with a groan. "Pain is weakness leaving the body. There's always some weakling standing in the shadows of the strong. Now they're gone."

Oliver felt the blood drain from his face.

Juan walked over and hovered just inches away, "What's the matter? Surprised your trinkets didn't work as you thought?"

Juan stood up and dropped the bottle. He took his knife and shredded Oliver's shirt from him.

Oliver pleaded, "You don't have to do this."

Juan smiled and winked at Oliver, "Sure, I do."

Oliver's body became a wall of fire. Each cut added a flame. Blood began to drip onto the concrete. The room spun, and his strength began to waver. Soon, he could no longer feel the blade. The light in the room faded, and the man on the wall blurred.

Juan stepped back, "You're much stronger than I thought you'd be. I figured you'd have passed out a long time ago. I'm impressed. I have just two more cuts to make."

Oliver gasped. The blade slid down his chest bone. Then Juan made a horizontal cut, careful not to slip off the ribs. He took two steps back. His hands dripped with blood. Juan smiled and nodded his head in approval, "There, from me to you. You like your crosses. Well, now you have one for life."

Oliver let his head droop. He could just make out the deeper cuts. It looked like a T, and then he realized it was a cross over his heart. Blood oozed freely, creating a new trail over his pants and onto the chair.

Oliver blubbered, "What, what about my friends? Where are they?"

Juan shrugged, "Beats me. I disconnected their cameras, so I doubt they know I'm here."

****

Jaimie stared at the screens. Something was off. She backed up the video for the third time and then saw it.

She picked up her phone and called Robert, "Where are you?"

Robert's voice was chipper, "Just heading back from fishing. I have work tomorrow."

"You have to get here now. Juan's here."

"You're at Hollister House?"

Jaimie answered, "No, next door, but he's there. Hurry."

She dialed Jim and David. They both said they would be there in minutes and to keep the doors locked.

****

Oliver could feel his strength fading. His voice was weak, "I'm not sure I'll make it."

Juan waved his hand, "Oh well, them's the breaks."

Juan stumbled backward, and a deep voice came forth, "No!"

He rushed over to Oliver and examined the wounds, "This isn't allowed—that fool. I warned him. He could ruin everything. I should never trust a human."

Oliver let his head flop back, "What's wrong, demon, can't you control your puppet?"

Juan's hand grabbed Oliver by the hair, and sulfur filled his nostrils as the demon spoke through Juan, "What is it with you, humans? You think you're so special. You're dust, nothing else."

Oliver replied, "We're the image of God."

Juan's hand released his hair, and he began to pace, "Ha! You look nothing like our Creator. You're a poor imitation, and because He thought you were beautiful and we disagreed, we've been banished from His presence."

"That's on you."

Sulfur-filled air hovered around Oliver. "What would you know? Were you around when He created the universe? We were. We once laughed and rejoiced in His presence with the other angels. Then He made you. We served the throne while you betrayed His love. How dare He tells us to serve His puppets of dust."

Oliver sighed, "Pride."

The chorus of demons responded, "Humans are the kings of pride."

Oliver answered, "I'm too tired to argue. I just want to sleep."

Juan collapsed and then got up from the ground, "Okay. I have bandages. I can't let you die and ruin everything."

Juan went behind Oliver and returned with rolls of gauze. He fumbled with Oliver's arm, which was still tied to the armrest.

David's familiar voice hollered, "Get away from him!"

Oliver looked in his direction. He saw Robert aiming his revolver, "Freeze."

Juan twitched, and a chorus of demon laughter filled the room.

David stepped forward, "You can't defeat us, demons."

He charged across the room and put the cross on Juan's chest, but nothing happened. Oliver could see fear in David's eyes for the first time. Juan grabbed the cross and tossed it to the side. He shoved David, who lost his footing and slid to the other side of the room.

Jim pulled out two bottles of holy water and flung them toward the fully possessed Juan. Juan gave a blood-curdling cackle and pretended to shower.

David yelled, "Everyone, rush him."

The group tried to move but couldn't. They remained held in place. The revolver clanked against the concrete. Oliver tried to wiggle his weakened arm free as Juan walked over and stared at each person individually. They looked away. Jaimie shuddered. Juan returned to Oliver and pulled out his knife.

He cut Oliver's legs and arms loose. Oliver tried to stand but collapsed back into the chair. He reached up and felt the deep cuts over his heart.

Juan's voice had returned, "This changes things. I can't leave your friends unscathed. Perhaps I should kill someone, just so you know I'm serious. Let's see, what about the cop who arrested me."

Oliver's eyes widened, "You said nobody was going to die."

"I think I've changed my mind."

Juan started towards the team, frozen in place.

Oliver yelled, "No! The demons won't let you."

Juan turned, "I do what I want. Tell me, Gringo. Who dies?"

Oliver's fingers traced over his blood, and he wiped it on the side of his face.

Juan rolled his eyes, "I don't have time for this."

Oliver looked at Juan, "It's the blood."

"What?"

"It's not the holy water, the crucifix, or me. It's the blood of Christ."

Juan pointed at Oliver, "You're hysterical. That's your blood."

Oliver nodded, "Yea, this isn't about my blood, theirs, or yours."

Juan's body convulsed, and a chorus screamed, "You can't know."

Oliver noticed his friends began to move. Robert grabbed his revolver off the ground and fired two shots. Juan's body shuddered with the impact. He turned to Robert and growled, "Thanks for the soul."

Oliver forced himself up and leaned against the arm of the chair, "I am a child of God." He pointed to his friends, "So are they. The blood of Jesus adopts us. We have the authority in the name of Jesus, and we banish you. You will never return to this or any other place. Go to the abyss where you belong."

The ground shook, and Oliver fell into the chair. Juan's possessed body lurched, jerked, spun, and collapsed to the ground. The house's frame began to shake, and light filled the basement windows. The chorus of demons screamed, and the body convulsed.

The screams got louder, and a light blinded Oliver. He covered his ears and closed his eyes, but the defensive posture seemed useless. The screams and light left him feeling deaf and dumb for a few moments. Then, the room got quiet. He opened his eyes to see Jaimie getting to her feet.

He attempted to stand to meet her, but the room spun, and everything went black.

Chapter Twenty-One

Bright light flooded around Oliver. The pain, weakness, and nausea he was feeling disappeared. His bright surroundings began to fade away, and he found himself back where he met the messenger.

"Hello? Is anyone else here?"

There was no answer. Oliver looked around and then started walking. Nothing changed, so he kept going, unsure of his destination. In the far distance, he could make out green hills and trees. Oliver quickened his pace. A building started coming into view that he thought he recognized, and he began to run.

The ground beneath his feet turned into grass. He stopped, and his jaw dropped open. In front of him sat his old high school. It glistened clean and new in the sun. A familiar voice caught his attention.

"Beautiful, isn't it? This old place never looked so good."

Oliver turned to find Tracy walking toward him.

"Tracy, but, but, you're dead."

Tracy laughed, "Do I look dead? Oh, you mean in the old world? Yea, you could say that."

Oliver's forehead creased, "I don't understand. Wait, you mean I'm dead? Is this heaven?"

Tracy raised his hands, "Whoa, slow down there, Ollie. If you think this is heaven, you have a pretty low opinion of the place. You're not dead. You're only mostly dead."

"You mean like in the movie?"

Tracy smiled, "Sort of. Juan was a violent man and not very skilled. Those flesh wounds went a bit deeper than he thought. Your life is hanging on by a thread."

Oliver crossed his arms, "Wait, how do you know about Juan?"

"You know you can't ask the dead those questions."

Oliver responded, "You just said you aren't dead. Besides, I'm not the one who came looking for you."

Tracy answered, "No, you're not. I'm here under special dispensation from God. I thought the old high school would bring back some fond memories. You know, before we grew up, and then I left."

"Did you have a choice?"

Tracy answered, "Does anyone?"

Oliver looked down at the perfectly cut grass, "No."

"Good, you have learned something. Let me ask you a question, was the pain worth it?"

Oliver dropped his arms to his side and cocked his head. "You mean with Juan?"

Tracy nodded.

"I don't know. I was hoping he would accept Jesus and the demons leave. So, I sort of feel like maybe all this was for nothing."

Tracy's eyes looked straight at Oliver, "What about what you learned?"

Oliver looked at the perfectly blue sky and down at the emerald grass. His eyes brightened, "Oh, well, knowing who I am to God. Yes, I guess that was worth it. After all, look at me now. I'm healed."

Tracy chuckled, "Not exactly."

"What do you mean?"

Tracy answered, "Let's say when you get back, you won't be feeling this good. Don't worry. You'll fully recover, but it'll be a few months."

"Months!"

"Juan almost skinned you alive. You don't just walk away from that."

The corner of Oliver's mouth turned down, "Well, I guess I don't have a choice. Why did you want to know if it was worth it?"

Tracy walked over and put his arm around Oliver's shoulder. It felt like they were kids talking about kid drama at school again, "I want you to understand that I hated cancer. The chronic pain, losing control over my life. I hated all of it. But, I drew close to Jesus. By the time I got to heaven, I felt like I'd come home. That part of my life on earth was horrible, but it was worth it in the end. Not everyone has to suffer to get that close to our Creator, but I guess I did. I hope that makes sense."

Oliver turned to Tracy, "Yea. Thankfully, you'll never have to worry about pain again. It sounds like that isn't the case for me."

Tracy removed his arm and stepped back, "Keep the faith."

A wind picked up. The world seemed to melt away and turn gray. Tracy shot skyward and disappeared in a moment. Oliver's skin felt like it was burning. He stumbled, fell to his knees, closed his eyes, and tried to breathe. He felt something covering his mouth and grabbed at it.

Oliver opened his eyes. A dim room with one fluorescent bulb turned on surrounded him. Jaimie's beautiful face looked at him with red and puffy eyes. She smiled and buried her head into his chest.

Burning pain danced where her nose and lips landed, and Oliver gasped.

She sat up, "I'm sorry. We just, I just, well, the doctors weren't sure you'd wake up."

"How long have I been sleeping?"

Jaimie adjusted Oliver's oxygen mask and then held his hand, "Sleeping. Honey, they had you in an induced coma for the last two weeks to give your body time to recover from the trauma."

"Two weeks? I was only with Tracy for a few minutes."

Jaimie squeezed his hand tighter, "You saw Tracy? Oh, we did almost lose you."

"Do my mom and dad know?"

Jaimie nodded, "They're at your place, resting. They stayed here at the hospital the entire first week. David finally convinced them they needed to get some rest."

Oliver smiled, "Sounds like David. I guess he never doubted."

Jaimie shook her head, "When they put you in the ambulance, he had tears in his eyes. He kept mumbling about a cost."

"Yea. There's a cost to fighting demons. I think this time, we all paid the price. How did you know I was in the basement? Juan said the cameras were unplugged down there."

Jaimie answered, "It was a combination of the other cameras and divine intervention. I was next door the whole time you were in the basement and didn't even realize it. I could have never forgiven myself if you had died. Anyway, I was looking at the camera footage from around the house. Juan was careful but not careful enough.

"One camera on the ground floor was facing the kitchen window. I saw him peak inside the house. It was just minutes before the basement camera went off. I called everyone, and we came over together. By God's grace, we got there when we did."

Oliver asked, "How's Robert? You know, after shooting Juan."

"David and Jim have spent some serious time with Robert. He's a believer, but life as a policeman sure did make him cynical. We invited him to church, and he started attending. We'll see, but the experience seems to have made him softer instead of harder."

The sound of the door opening caught Oliver's attention. A nurse walked into the room, "I see our patient is awake. Were the two of you going to keep it a secret or let me know?"

Jaimie blushed, "I'm sorry. I was overwhelmed."

The nurse walked over and took Oliver's hand, "Don't worry. I would be the same way if it were my husband."

Both answered in unison, "We aren't married."

The nurse smiled, "Yet. You aren't married yet."

Oliver and Jaimie blushed. Oliver's arm jerked, and the nurse gripped him tighter, "I'm sorry, but I have to check the dressing."

He finally looked down for the first time. Both arms were covered in gauze and tape. It ran from his wrists to inside his hospital gown. "How many stitches?"

"I'm too lazy to use stitches."

Oliver looked towards the door again. A petite woman with long, straight brown hair, brown skin, and dark eyes stood at the doorway.

"I'm Dr. Hunter. You had so many cuts we would have been sewing for days. You're fortunate to be alive in this day and age. We glued you back together."

Oliver asked, "How long will I have to be in the hospital?"

"Well, I want you here for at least a few more days. We need to give your body time to recover from the coma. Please do me a favor. Raise both arms in front of you."

The nurse released his hand, and she and Jaimie stepped back. Oliver tried to raise his arms. They felt like lead. He focused and forced them upward. Stabbing pain shot through his muscles, and his skin burned.

Dr. Hunter spoke up, "Okay, stop, put them down."

Oliver lowered his arms.

"Nurse, lower the guard rail."

The nurse complied.

"Try to sit up."

Oliver attempted to sit up, but dizziness overcame him, and he barely got his back off the bed.

Dr. Hunter nodded, "Well, the good news is that you are exactly where I expected you to be. The bad news is that it will be at least two more days before you can go home, maybe as long as another week. That's assuming your wife can take care of you."

Jaimie responded, "Oh, I'm not his wife."

"Do you live together?"

"No."

Oliver spoke up, "My parents are at my house. They can help."

Dr. Hunter asked, "How long will they be there?"

"I don't know."

Dr. Hunter walked over to Oliver's bed and spoke in a quieter tone, "Oliver, let me explain what has happened. Your body has gone through a major trauma. It will take time to heal, both physically and mentally. It will be at least a couple of months, maybe longer. If you don't have anyone who can stay with you, I'll talk to your insurance company about at-home care."

Oliver looked over at Jaimie, "What's Jim up to now?"

Jaimie answered, "Working at home and waiting on my phone call. Between him and David, we've got you covered."

Oliver said, "Well, Jim will probably be enough."

Dr. Hunter responded, "I want the names and phone numbers of the people caring for you. My nurse will be making phone calls and getting updates."

Jaimie and Oliver nodded.

The doctor spent the next few minutes reading Oliver's chart and checking the cuts under his dressing. When she finished, she started to leave the room but turned and spoke, "You're going to have a lot of scars."

Oliver nodded, "I know. I've seen what it looks like."

The doctor gave him a confused look, and she and the nurse walked out of the room.

Chapter Twenty-Two

Oliver opened his eyes. Juan's twisted face was just inches from his.

"Did you think you could escape me so easily? I hope you enjoyed your little nap. That will be your last. Well, unless I change my mind."

Oliver jerked to get his arms and feet free. The chair jumped around the floor. Dark shadows danced on the walls of the basement. The yellowish lightbulb flashed, and a hideous laugh filled the air.

Juan pressed against the cuts on Oliver's chest, and a ghoulish voice asked, "Do you like my handiwork?"

Black blood oozed down his chest into the pool of dark liquid on the floor. A blade flickered before his eye. Oliver pushed his head back. He tried to kick the chair out from under him. Juan grabbed his hair and pulled until he was sure it would all come out by the roots.

Juan whispered in his ear, "It's better to enter heaven with one good eye."

Oliver began to weep. A woman's voice spoke in his other ear, "Why didn't you listen to me?"

Juan released Oliver and stepped back. Melissa walked into view. She wore a thin blue laced dress that left little to the imagination, "I told you not to come back here. Now, look at you. Here you are, in your darkest hour, desiring to go back, desiring me. Your heart is deceptive. Perhaps Juan should cut it out."

Juan walked over and put his bloody arm around Melissa, "Should I?"

Melissa giggled and gleefully clapped her hands.

Oliver felt Juan's blade, and his chest ached. He closed his eyes and screamed. When he opened his eyelids, he found himself tangled in his bedsheets. Sweat dripped from his forehead. His chest hurt, but the bandages looked undamaged. He kicked off his covers and sat up on the edge of the bed.

His skin burned randomly in spots. Oliver eased himself off the bed and stumbled to his bathroom. He reached for his pain medicine, downed a pill, and then turned and leaned against the bathroom door.

His alarm clock showed five in the morning. Oliver shook his head, slowly made his way to the kitchen, and turned on the light. A few quick breaths were his only reward when he reached for the coffee in the cabinet. Pain, bandages, and weakness kept him just inches from his goal.

Jim's familiar voice spoke up behind him, "You know, I'm here to help with that. Go sit down, and I'll bring you a cup."

Oliver kept his eyes on the floor as he passed by Jim. He collapsed on the couch, tried to cross his arms, but then let them drop to his side. A few minutes later, Jim arrived with his coffee and sat next to him on the couch.

"Nightmare, huh?"

Oliver turned wide-eyed to Jim, "How did you know?"

"Remember, I've been shot before."

Oliver returned to his coffee, took a long sip, and gently cradled the mug, "How long do these last? I had a couple in the hospital, but I thought after they released me, they'd stop."

Jim made a comfortable spot in the corner of the couch and looked at Oliver, "You won't like this. Mine have never gone away. Oh, they get better and morph into other dreams. Not everything is a nightmare. Some people may not even have nightmares. My experience is mine. Who knows, you may be fine in a few days."

Oliver took another sip, adjusted his legs, and let the mug rest on the couch between his thighs. "The shrinks seem to think it'll take longer. I have some medicine; ever take yours?"

Jim nodded, "All the time. At first, I didn't. You know, tough cop and all of that. After a week with no sleep, I soon realized that I wasn't that tough."

Oliver sighed, "Okay. I'll keep taking mine. Juan is dead. There's no reason to let him live in my head."

"Good choice. Hey, any ideas on what you'll do when you heal up? I mean, besides going back to work."

Oliver smiled, "I thought I might do some ring shopping."

Jim smacked the top of the couch, "You, dog. Good for you."

"You're so sure she'll say yes?"

Jim rolled his eyes, "Stop it. Nobody could love you more than Jaimie."

Oliver's smile grew wider across his reddening face. "From your lips to God's ear."

"What else do you have in mind?"

Oliver finished his coffee and handed the mug to Jim. "You mean besides changing my whole life? Not much."

"Are you going to keep investigating with us?"

Oliver answered, "I mean, that depends on Jaimie, but yea, I'm planning on it."

"Good. I didn't know, you know, what with all that's happened."

Oliver stood up, "This? This was as much Juan as the demons. Besides, I know who I am and who we are in the eyes of God. If I can help somebody, I will. If you'll excuse me, I'm gonna get dressed."

Oliver eased his way back to his bedroom and tried to open the drawers to his dresser but failed.

Jim spoke up, "I thought you'd need a hand again. Look, take it easy for the next couple of weeks. Anything you need, tell me, and I'll get it for you."

"Ok. I'm still not used to accepting help."

Jim walked over and gently put his hand on Oliver's shoulder, "I wish I had accepted help when I was shot. Who knows, maybe I would have ended up in a different place. Take it from me, enjoy the help and the break from work. You'll be up and living your life again before you know it."

"I thought Tracy helped you out."

Jim answered, "He did, but that was after I had given up on being a cop anymore. By the time Tracy sat me down, I was ready to give up on life. We talked about our purpose in the world, and then he talked me into trying computers. I found the work fun, and it brought me back into your world and Jaimie's. Heck, I'm even glad I met David."

Oliver sat down on his bed, "Okay, I'll accept this for now. Tell you what, why don't you draw me a bath Jeeves and then fold my laundry."

Both men started to laugh, and then tears began to roll down Oliver's cheeks. Jim sat down, put his arm around Oliver, and Oliver buried his head in Jim's chest.

Jim started slowly rocking back and forth, "Don't worry, you'll be okay."

About Author

Gary McPherson (1966-) was born in Sacramento, California, and spent his childhood in Westminster, Ca. For most of his adult life, Gary has lived in North Carolina. He and his wife have lived in Charlotte, NC, for thirty-one years. A change in health and a love of storytelling moved Gary from a 27-year career in Computer and Software Engineering to author of thrillers and humorous short stories. His Berserker series consists of, "Joshua and the Shadow of Death," "Harold and the Angel of Death," and "Bill and the Sting of Death." Also, Gary has written two short humorous anthologies under the pen name Lucius McCray. The first is titled "Country Boy." Lucius McCray's second book, "Humor Deeper Than a Holler," Lucius McCray's third book, "Humor Through The Ages" He also wrote a Vella paranormal mystery series "Unwanted Guest" on Amazon. He converted his story into a book in 2023. You can find guest articles by Gary in Writer's Digest, Criminal Element, Crimespree, Magazine, and Patient Worthy. You can find more information about Gary's books on his website:

https://luciusmccray.com/

Also By